THE PROMISE OF PEACE

D0366326

THE
PROMISE
OF PEACE

JEAN GRANT

Publishers Since 1798

THOMAS NELSON PUBLISHERS

Nashville • Atlanta • London • Vancouver

Published in Nashville, Tennessee, by Thomas Nelson, Inc., Publishers, and distributed in Canada by Word Communications, Ltd., Richmond, British Columbia, and in the United Kingdom by Word (UK), Ltd., Milton Keynes, England.

Scripture quotations are from the NEW KING JAMES VERSION of the Bible. Copyright © 1979, 1980, 1982, Thomas Nelson, Inc., Publishers.

Library of Congress Cataloging-in-Publication Data

Grant, Jean.
The promise of peace / Jean Grant
p. cm. — (Salinas Valley saga)
ISBN 0–7852–8104–5
I. Title. II. Series: Grant, Jean. Salinas Valley saga.
PS3557.R2663P75   1995
813'.54—dc20   94–24854
                                                      CIP

Printed in the United States of America
1 2 3 4 5 6 7 - 01 00 99 98 97 96 95

Prologue

Marianne Hanlon was a striking young woman. Heads turned as she found her seat in the railway car and removed the plain navy blue poke bonnet she wore, stowing it in the overhead rack. She was quite tall and fashionably slender, though nothing else about her could be called fashionable.

Her navy serge suit was cut plainly, almost military in style, which was hardly surprising given the red Salvation Army emblem that brightened its high collar. Her hair, which glistened coppery red in the sunlight, was pulled back primly into a bun at the nape of her neck, with only a very few, very stubborn curls struggling for freedom.

But nothing could control her eyes. They were aquamarine, the color of Monterey Bay on a crystal clear day, and they were as deep as the channel cut into that bay by the Salinas River. She was on her way back from San Francisco, back to the river and the fertile valley it watered, back home to Soledad.

People looked at her and smiled, and she returned their smiles warmly, as if each were an old friend. The corners of her mouth twitched and her eyes twinkled as she played a *favorite game.* What were they thinking as they smiled at her?

The young mother whispered something to her small children and pointed. Marianne caught the words, ". . . help poor people."

A stout middle-aged man in a business suit felt for his wallet. He expects me to ask him for a donation. She pressed her lips together and suppressed a chuckle.

A pair of teenaged girls peeked over the fashion magazine they were thumbing and frowned. Did they expect a sermon?

A too-thin young woman with flushed cheeks coughed into her handkerchief, and Marianne automatically ticked off the symptoms.

There was a young man whose gaze seemed appraising but not unappreciative. Modesty wouldn't permit Marianne to read his thoughts as he shrugged and returned to his newspaper.

The train pulled out of the Townsend Street Station and chugged slowly through the city. It would take all day to travel the nearly 150 miles to Soledad with all the stops in between.

These two places she loved were worlds apart. San Francisco was a bustling, cosmopolitan city riding the crest of the Roaring Twenties. The Salinas Valley where Marianne had grown up was a long, twisting rift between the Santa Lucia and Gavilan mountains. It was a place of black furrowed soil and bright green growing things, an expanse of sprawling farms and tiny villages.

This trip would take a long time, but soon Marianne would be taking a much longer trip. In just a few months, perhaps, she would be going to a place she could barely imagine. She pulled a crisply typed letter from her handbag: her orders.

She'd have two short weeks with her family and then meet her friend Jade in San Francisco's Chinatown. Soon, her Salvation Army superiors believed, it would be safe to send workers to southern China. In the meantime, she could acquaint herself further with the language and customs of the Chinese while working among the needy in California.

She had asked to go to China, had dreamed of it for the past long five years. Lord, she silently prayed, let me serve you well here or there, and let me be content.

She had fulfilled her first dream of becoming a nurse. And that summer six years ago, she had decided to join the Salvation Army. God had then used her new friend Jade to introduce her to China. Mysterious Jade, born in Shanghai, was torn with a silent terror when Marianne first met her in Oakland. She had slowly become Marianne's close friend and, like her, was now a Salvation Army officer.

But I was going to China with Paul. *Marianne's smile faded as she gazed from the train window.* Maybe . . . *She tried not to hope, fearing her hope betrayed. He was going to China, too, he'd said, but to a village in the interior. But he was going alone. He loved her, he had said, but she had hurt him so. Now they were both going to China, but not together.*

I won't think about Paul, *she told herself, but she couldn't brush aside the sadness. She glanced again at the young mother across the aisle.* Oh, God, why may I not have a husband, children, love?

Adele was getting married next week, Marianne reminded herself, and she was scarcely conscious of the shiver that she felt. Most young women relished the excitement and the romance of a wedding, but weddings brought back memories.

Marianne pushed the fear back into the farthest recesses of her mind and was happy for Adele's joy.

Marianne and Adele had grown up together in Fort Romie, the tiny cluster of church, grange hall, and general store a few miles out of Soledad. Technically, Adele was Marianne's aunt, half-sister to Marianne's mother, Carrie McLean Hanlon. But the girls were only a few days apart in age and were fast friends.

It was surprising, in a way, that Adele hadn't been married for several years already. When we were girls . . . Marianne smiled, remembering the whispered confidences they'd shared so often. They had both been so carefree that last summer, giggly high school girls, eagerly anticipating boyfriends, dates, and weddings.

Marianne admitted that she had been a little more mature even then, and, yes, more popular. But Adele was pretty, too, in her soft, blonde way, and such a flirt. That summer, right after the war, they were happily certain that their lives would follow the normal Salinas Valley pattern. They would go to parties and picnics with the valley boys, and after high school there would be a natural pairing off followed by weddings. Then each couple would set up housekeeping on a piece of his father's farm.

Adele had broken the pattern too. Why? Marianne wondered. Could it possibly have had anything to do with what happened to me? She shrugged off the idea. Maybe Adele was just bored with the boys she'd known all her life. Marianne had always suspected Adele's sudden decision to go to normal school in San Jose was at least partly due to Anna's ambition for her children.

Anna, Adele's mother and Marianne's step-grandmother, was a wise woman. Hadn't she even sent Marianne's mother, Carrie, off to San Francisco right after Anna and Sam McLean married? Anna and Carrie had always been close, so Anna wasn't trying to get rid of her new stepdaughter. No, she had known Carrie could not be happy in the valley until she had been away from it.

Marianne nodded absently. The bookish schoolteacher Adele was marrying would hardly have appealed to the girl Marianne had known so well. Yet Adele was ecstatic. And it was romantic, Marianne thought, the way he had taken the job in Salinas to be near Adele and court her after they had graduated from the normal school in San Jose.

Yes, she was happy for Adele and Donald. But thinking of them rubbed the ache in her own heart. Marianne didn't want to think about Paul, but he was always there. Can I really serve God better alone? Is that why the Lord put my life on this pathway that is so different from the one I dreamed about as a girl?

The train took a young woman back to Soledad, but in her mind, Marianne became a fifteen-year-old again. Yes, that was when her path had turned, that day just after the war ended, that April day in 1919 when her uncles had returned from France.

Chapter One

The excited bunch of kids bounced along the rutted dirt road in the Sears Roebuck truck bed that had been welded onto the McLean's sturdy black Model T Ford. It was a warm, sunny Friday afternoon in April. School was out, and they were going home to Fort Romie, named for the Salvation Army farm colony that used to be there. But today the Hanlons and McLeans were going to stop in Soledad on the way to welcome the first of Fort Romie's soldiers back from the war.

Marianne Hanlon explained to Bill, who had lived in the Salinas Valley for only a few months, just who her family was expecting on the train from San Francisco. "Your uncles?" he asked. Adele said they were her brothers. "Does that mean Adele's your aunt?"

"Sure. Didn't you know that?" Marianne laughed that tinkling, bright, contagious laugh that made her such fun to be with. "Auntie, explain it to him."

Adele, a plump, blue-eyed blonde who didn't look related to Marianne, and certainly didn't seem old enough to be her best friend's aunt, giggled. "It's simple. Eric Arnesen is my brother on my mother's side. Tim McLean is my brother on my father's side. They're the same age, and they are best friends, just like Marianne and I are best friends."

"But she's still Marianne's aunt," Joanie interjected.

"My mother is Tim's older sister," Marianne explained. "Their mother died when Tim was a baby and later, much later, their father married Eric's mother, who was a widow. Then they had my Uncle Harry," she waved at the youthful driver of the Ford, "and my Aunt Adele. See, it's simple."

Bill groaned. "Oh. Well, they've been to war, and now they're coming home. What difference does it make who's related to whom? They'll have lots of stories about France."

The young people in the truck jostled against each other as Harry brought the Model T to a lurching stop across from the railroad station. Bill jumped down, and Harry and his friend George hopped out of the cab. Joanie scrambled from the truck on her own, but Harry helped his sister, Adele, while George offered a hand to Marianne.

Next year, when I'm a junior, Marianne thought, *maybe George will ask to bring me into town some Saturday. He could take me to a Charlie Chaplin matinee at the local movie house and buy me a soda at the ice cream parlor.* Dad had said, "Maybe, when you're sixteen," and she would be sixteen next September.

Soledad was growing. It had lost out to Gonzales, fifteen miles north, as the site for the new high school they attended, but the wooden sidewalk along Front Street was crowded. People shopped and visited inside the Soledad Mercantile. In the genteel dining room of the Head Hotel, waiters were already setting tables for supper. Farm folks ate early.

As their three friends waved and started for their homes, the youngest McLeans and Marianne joined their mothers, who beckoned them from the depot platform.

Carrie Hanlon was slim, like her oldest daughter, despite having had three children, but Carrie lacked Marianne's vivid coloring. She was nearing forty, and twenty years of farming the Salinas Valley had tanned her fair skin and faded her light brown hair. But she still carried her head as proudly as she had as a girl, and her brown eyes swept the lush valley through lustrous lashes.

Anna McLean was only about ten years older than her stepdaughter, but her braided hair, worn in a crown above her broad brow, had turned from gold to silver. Sam McLean had died that past winter of influenza, so Anna wore widow's black again. She gave Adele a quick hug, not turning her eyes from the northbound railroad track.

"Aren't they here yet?" Adele asked. "Harry was hurrying because we thought you'd all be waiting for us."

"The train's late. The station master says it will be here in fifteen minutes or so."

"Didn't Dad come?" Marianne asked her mother.

"No, and I'm glad he didn't." Carrie laughed. "He'd be chomping at the bit if he'd had to wait this long." Marianne's father, Matt, was not a patient man.

3

"He's planting the last of the sugar beets," Anna said, glancing at her son.

"I told him I'd help him with that tomorrow," Harry protested. "I know how much work he has this year with Papa gone."

"Matt didn't want you to miss your baseball game, Harry," Carrie explained. "You'll be working hard enough, come summer."

"But Carrie, Matt has all your land to look after and the old Russell place he and Sam bought last fall," objected Anna. Tears glittered in her pale blue eyes. "Matt can't tend to my farm too. I'm sorry, Harry, but I'm afraid there won't be much time for baseball this summer. Maybe when Eric is well."

"Tim will be out of his khakis and into his overalls in no time, Anna," Carrie reminded her. "Eric can take it easy this year and get his strength back."

Marianne would never have admitted it, but the thought of having a sick veteran to care for was exhilarating. She listened attentively as Anna discussed her son's illness with Carrie.

"Eric writes that he's feeling better all the time. And the fresh air and sunshine should be just what he needs."

"Sure, Ma," Harry assured her. "Lots of boys were gassed. Most of them are doing just fine."

"I do hope and pray he will recover completely." Anna sighed as she glanced toward Nancy Johnson, who had been waiting beside the family group. "It may take Tim a while to get back into the harness."

Nancy was a pretty woman, a bit too buxom for the current fashion, soft and rounded. Her gentle face was framed by short, blonde waves. She smiled as she stared down the railroad track, but her fingers fiddled with her beaded handbag. Marianne and Adele exchanged knowing winks as they turned to her.

"Have you picked out the patterns for our dresses yet, Nancy?"

She jumped, startled from her thoughts by the question. "Oh, the dresses. No, not yet."

"But you're getting married right away, aren't you?" Adele insisted. "And you said we could be bridesmaids."

"You will be, I promise." Nancy smiled then. "But we haven't even set a date. Tim only proposed the day before he left, and maybe he'll want a little time to get settled before we get married."

"I'll bet he won't," Adele answered, giggling. "Oh, it's so exciting. I can't wait to be old enough to have beaus and get married. Can you, Marianne?"

"I guess not," Marianne agreed. "Weddings are thrilling, and everyone wants to get married, but, you know, I think I'd like to do something else first, like you did, Nancy."

"Do you want to be a teacher, Marianne? It's aggravating sometimes."

"I think maybe I'd like to be a nurse," Marianne replied thoughtfully. "I don't mind taking care of sick people, and I'd like to be able to help people feel better."

"Ugh!" Adele exclaimed. "Why would anyone want to spend her life in such nasty places as hospitals? Especially," she winked at her best friend, "when someone as handsome as George Pelham was seen carrying her books to class the other day."

"Oh, George. He's such a tease," Marianne protested, her fair skin blushing.

They all jumped as the train whistle sounded in the distance. Nancy hesitated a little as the others bunched on the platform and stared excitedly at the approaching engine.

"Where are they? Where are they, anyhow?" Adele demanded, jumping up and down as the train slowed. Marianne hung back a bit shyly, while Anna and Carrie anxiously searched the windows of the passenger cars.

Nancy joined the knot of family, still twisting the strings of her handbag as the train crawled to a stop. "There!" She pointed to a strapping young man in uniform who had jumped from one of the cars and had reached up to help his friend, a gaunt, pale figure whose khakis hung loosely from his sagging shoulders.

Anna caught her breath. "He said he was better," she murmured. "He said he'd be fine, but he looks so terribly frail."

Eric had always been slender but tough, wiry, and agile like his father, Harold Arnesen. Marianne recalled he had always seemed to be in a hurry. But now he leaned heavily on the arm of his stepbrother.

Anna reached them first and surrounded her son with her strong arms, cuddling him to her ample breast as if to nurture him. Harry stood back until his mother loosened her grip. Then he put an arm around his half brother.

Tim, after releasing Eric to Anna, reached eager arms out to Nancy, who clung to him, hiding her face in his shoulder. "Oh, Tim!" she whispered. "Oh, Tim, thank God you're safe."

Marianne was enchanted by the young lovers. She noticed Nancy's eyes fill as she glanced toward, and quickly away from, Eric. *Of course she feels sorry for him. She did go with him for a while before the war. But she and Tim are obviously so much in love.*

Eric had seen Nancy, too, but he turned away from the couple's embrace. "Carrie," he said hoarsely.

He stretched out a trembling hand and Carrie took it saying, "Welcome home."

Eric forced a teasing smile as he looked at Adele and Marianne. "Don't tell me these pretty young ladies are my kid sister and my little niece. I've only been away a year, and you two are all grown up."

Chapter Two

A dusty Fordson tractor stood in its shed. Marianne's brother Ted, who was in the eighth grade at nearby Mission School, had been cleaning the heavy Salinas Valley adobe from the plow. He straightened up and waved as his mother drove the family Studebaker into the yard. The McLeans' Model T truck turned in behind her.

"They're here!" the boy shouted, brushing the mud from the legs of his overalls. Lizzie, his ten-year-old sister, dashed out of the house and Matt followed.

"I just finished plucking a couple of chickens," Matt told his wife and oldest daughter as he reached out a strong earth-stained hand to his brother-in-law. "Tim, it's great to have you home. You're looking fit. Are you just about ready to get back to work?"

Matt's eyes twinkled as he noticed Nancy, who still clung to Tim's arm. "Though I can probably wait longer than she will," he added in a stage whisper.

Anna and Harry had gotten out of the Model T and were helping Eric to the ground. Matt grasped his wife's hand as he tried not to stare at the shattered invalid. He had never been good at hiding his feelings, but he struggled now to be cheerful. "And Eric," he bluffed, taking a couple of giant steps to greet the young man he'd known since Eric was a little boy. "Eric, it's good to see you. Looks like you really need some of our sunshine and your ma's good home cooking."

"That's just what I need, Matt." Eric nodded; his hand shook as it met Matt's. "I guess you've had your hands full since Pa McLean died, but I mean to take on my share again right away."

"Oh, there's no hurry. You just wait until you're up to it. Why, Will and I have been doing just fine this spring, and now we'll have Tim too. And Harry and Ted will be out of school soon. That's plenty of hands to take care of things."

"Where is Will?" Eric glanced around the yard, looking for his other stepbrother. "I've sure missed that guy."

"He and Irene will be over after supper," Matt answered. "I told him yesterday when we were planting sugar beets that you'd be home today."

"Aunt Irene's been awfully busy with the new baby," Marianne explained. "But she'll be anxious to show him off to both of you, I'm sure."

"Another Sam McLean, I hear." Eric nodded. "Too bad he'll never know his grandpa."

"Pa spoiled our three," Carrie said sadly. "But I guess it's something special, having someone to carry on the name. Pa was looking forward to seeing his sons' sons."

9

"Looks like there'll be more McLeans soon," Eric observed flatly, as he watched Tim and Nancy sitting alone on the porch swing.

"Let's go inside and have a seat," Anna urged, and her sons followed her, the older leaning on the younger for strength.

There was nothing special about the Hanlon house. There were hundreds like it in the Salinas Valley—solid two-story frame houses with gabled ends and wide front porches. But the house was proof that Matt Hanlon was a successful farmer. A low wing extended off one end of the original two-room structure. It held the big country kitchen with its new gas stove and a new indoor bathroom. Broad dormers lighted the bedrooms that had pushed up the old roof to provide sleeping space as the family had grown.

Carrie whispered to Marianne as they went inside, "Would you please start dinner for me? Liz can help."

"Come on, Lizzie," Marianne grumbled as she reluctantly headed for the kitchen. "We have to fix dinner while the 'grown-ups' visit."

Marianne was already a good cook. She'd had two of the best teachers in the valley, her own mother and Anna, whom she called Gran. As much as Marianne wanted to stay in the cool parlor and listen to the war stories she was sure Tim and Eric were telling, she was proud to be trusted with dinner.

Her father had plucked and cleaned the fresh-killed young roosters. As she reached for a butcher knife to cut them into pieces for frying, she directed her sister, "Better peel lots of potatoes, and get some carrots from the root cellar to go with the peas. Uncle Eric needs lots of good vegetables."

"He looks awfully sick, doesn't he? And he has such a terrible cough too."

"That's the mustard gas. It makes your lungs all hard, so you can't breathe right."

"Is he going to die, like Grandpa?" Liz asked.

"Maybe." Marianne put the heavy cast iron skillet on the gas stove. "If he gets pneumonia. But he already had the flu, and he got over that." Marianne thought of how colorless Eric looked, his hair a washed-out yellow, his skin almost gray. "We have to see that he gets lots of good food and fresh air and sunshine."

"He won't be able to help Dad much, will he? Ted told me Dad was really counting on them. He told Ted that he and Grandpa probably shouldn't have bought the Russell place, but it was such a good deal."

"They couldn't have known that Grandpa was going to get sick. They wanted that farm for Tim, so Grandpa could leave his place to Eric one day."

Marianne looked out the kitchen window, past the whirring windmill. Everything as far as she could see was either Hanlon or McLean land—her father's farm, her Uncle Will's, the Russell place that was to be Tim's, and the acres Sam McLean had gradually acquired over the past twenty years. The wheat was already tall and bright emerald green, and the pasture grass shimmered in the breeze. The fields newly planted with sugar beets were corduroy black.

Marianne didn't know much about the rest of the world, but her father had told her over and over that right here in the Salinas Valley was the best place on earth to live. Sometimes the older folks talked about the hard times, when the McLeans first came to the valley, when Marianne's mother was an old-young eighteen.

There hadn't been any deep wells then, or any windmills to pump up the water. Those first years had been years of drought. People had carried water in barrels from the shallow surface flow of the Salinas River, not understanding that under the baked adobe lay one of the largest reservoirs of ground water in the world.

But the elder McLeans and Hanlons didn't talk overmuch about the hard years. They'd survived. They'd held on to that first ten acres bought on credit as part of the Salvation Army's Fort Romie experiment. Now they owned, between them, several hundred acres of deep black clay. It was hard to work but tremendously productive.

In the years before the war, when Marianne was a little girl, they'd always had enough to eat and extra money to buy more land. But when Europe began to destroy itself, the land brought forth wealth. During the past five years, the wheat and navy beans and sugar beets brought record prices. *Not that we're rich*, Marianne reminded herself, as her mother had often reminded her. *But praise God we have plenty, and plenty to share.* "And," she said aloud, startling her younger sister, "praise God the war is over and Uncle Tim and Uncle Eric are home again."

The supper table was stretched to its full length but was still crowded. Anna hovered over a quiet Eric near Matt's end of the table; Tim and Nancy seemed totally absorbed in each other at the other end despite a constant stream of questions from the young people clustered in between.

"Did you shoot any Germans, Uncle Tim?" Ted quizzed.

"I shot at some," Tim answered. "They weren't all that close, over in their trenches. We never knew if we hit any."

"What's Paris like, Tim?" Adele asked. "They say Frenchmen are so romantic."

"Oh, Adele," Marianne interrupted, "can't you think of anything but men?" She turned to her Uncle Tim. "War must be so awful. Did you see anyone get hurt?"

"A few. It's not much fun, but we did what we had to." Tim turned his attention back to Nancy.

Eric coughed weakly, and Marianne glanced at him and then looked down at her plate. "I think war must be the most horrible thing on earth," she said quietly. "How can God let men do such things to other men?"

"It's the devil that makes war, Marianne," Eric wheezed. "Out there you wonder if there even is a God, because if there were a God, surely he would put a stop to such madness."

"Well, it's over now." Anna filled a glass with fresh milk and handed it to her son. "Drink it," she urged. "It will bring your strength back."

"Yes, Mama." He smiled wanly. "You know, you're as bad as the nurses at the hospital."

"I'm going to be a nurse," Marianne told him proudly. "I helped when we had the influenza, and everybody said I was a born nurse."

"It's hard work, Marianne, but at least, God willing, you'll never see what those girls in France saw." Eric coughed again, and Marianne's deep blue eyes filled with tears of pity.

"That's enough war talk," Matt interrupted. "I expect the boys would rather think about the future than about the war."

As Eric finished his milk, Matt caught his eye. "Speaking of the future, Eric, I'd like to talk to you about your mother's farm sometime soon. Sam had planned to put in mostly wheat this spring. Beans went sky high the past couple of years, but with the war over we thought they might drop."

"The wheat crop looked good as we came past," Eric commented.

"Well, yes, the wheat's doing fine. But I left a few acres of land fallow. Some of us have been thinking about trying something new." Matt hesitated, and Harry jumped into the discussion.

"Eric, we've been experimenting at high school with truck crops. You wouldn't believe the way cabbage grows here. Why, we had five pound heads, lots of them, last year."

"Yup," Matt put in. "Never saw such cabbage and lettuce and carrots."

Eric tried to be interested. "But is there a market for vegetables?"

His brother was well prepared to answer. "San Francisco's bigger now than it was before the fire, and Oakland and Berkeley are just growing like crazy. We could ship stuff by overnight freight train and still get it there faster than from over in the Central Valley. Besides, our growing season is different from theirs. What with our cool summers, we can harvest in midsummer, when that kind of stuff just goes to seed from the heat over around Fresno and Stockton."

Matt nodded agreement. "Remember how Sam used to talk about growing vegetables and taking them to the city to sell? Well, that was before we had Ford trucks." His strong arm swept an arc across the table. "Now it should be easy. Harry wants to try a few acres and take them to market himself."

"Harry? At his age?"

Harry bristled at Eric's question.

But Harry wasn't much older when Eric left than I am now, Marianne realized.

"Harry's grown up a lot since you went away, Eric," Anna reminded him. "He graduates from high school in six weeks. And he's heard his pa talk about selling truck crops in the city since he was a toddler. Now it makes good sense."

Eric frowned, and Harry began to urge the project on him, but Anna continued. "You've just gotten home, Eric, and I can see you're tired. We don't have to decide tonight."

"What do you think, Tim?" Harry pressed. "I mean, it's partly your farm too. Don't you think we should try new things?"

"My farm too? Funny, I never thought of that place belonging to anyone but Pa." The three half brothers looked at each other. "I guess we do have some decisions to make, don't we?"

By the time they'd finished supper, Eric was obviously exhausted. Ted had finally cornered Tim for some war talk, so Anna turned to her youngest son and asked, "Harry, will you drive your brother and me home? Adele, why don't you stay and help Carrie with the dishes. You can walk home with Tim later."

"Shoo," Nancy waved the younger girls out of the kitchen when they had finished clearing the table. "I'll help Carrie wash the dishes."

Carrie nodded. "It's okay, girls. You did a good job with the cooking. Anyhow, it's late. You'd better go up and do your homework, Liz, and then go to bed." She anticipated Marianne's question. "Yes, you can gossip with Adele until Tim's ready to leave." Then she turned to Nancy and smiled. "I promise I'll send Ted to bed as soon as we finish the dishes, so you can have Tim back."

Marianne and Adele huddled on the porch swing. "Did you notice how Eric kept looking at Tim and Nancy?" Marianne whispered. "I'll bet he isn't over her yet."

"Yeah, I guess he was sweet on her before, but they weren't engaged, or anything like that," Adele answered. "If they were, Nancy would never have gone out with Tim, would she? I mean, nice girls just don't."

"All the same, he's really sad when he looks at her."

"They're so cute, Nancy and Tim." Adele giggled, then reflectively added, "Maybe Eric is jealous. After all, he doesn't have a girl now."

"And he's so sick too. I think Nancy's sort of sad too."

"Come on, now," Adele protested. "Why, she held hands with Tim all during supper."

"I know. I don't mean she isn't happy about Uncle Tim being home and being in love with her. But I think she feels sorry for Uncle Eric too." Marianne had read in the newspaper about the constant pain of the soldiers who had been gassed in the trenches. "Who wouldn't feel sorry for him?"

The rattle of Will's shiny new Chevy cut their talk short. Irene came up the steps cradling her baby in her arms, and Marianne reached out and took him. "Oh, see how much you've grown already," she exclaimed. "Come on, Sammy, smile for your cousin."

"Where's my kid brother?" Will boomed, following his wife onto the porch.

"I've been here for hours," Tim challenged from the doorway. "What's been keeping you?"

The brothers slapped each other on the back exuberantly.

"Gay Paree must have agreed with you, Timmy. Did you have a good time with the cancan girls while I was stuck here on the old farm?"

"Look who's talking." Tim glanced at the baby in Marianne's arms. "Looks like you did just fine for yourself while I was off making the world safe for democracy."

Their broad grins gave the lie to their banter. Marianne handed Sammy over to his Uncle Tim, and the baby exploded in an angry wail at the sight of the strange face.

Irene rescued her son, who stopped shrieking immediately. "Where's Eric?" Will asked, as Matt, Carrie, and Nancy joined them on the front porch.

"He went home with Anna and Harry," Matt said "He was pretty tired."

"Uncle Eric's still terribly sick," Marianne offered.

"Yes, Will, Eric's in bad shape," Tim explained. "I guess he wrote you folks that everything was fine, but he took a lot of that mustard gas."

"We knew he'd been gassed, Tim, but none of us were prepared to see him like this. Did the doctors tell you anything about what to expect?" Carrie asked.

"I don't think they really know much about it," Tim said. "When I heard he was in the hospital I got leave to go see him. They weren't sure then that he'd even make it. He'd got the flu, and most of the ones that were gassed bad couldn't fight off the flu."

"But he got over that, and even pneumonia," Marianne observed. "At the Chautauqua they said the soldiers who had been gassed needed lots of rest and fresh air and good food."

"He will get well, won't he?" Nancy pleaded.

"Maybe," Tim answered. "But maybe not. The doctors said his lungs are half eaten away. He could get pneumonia again, or TB."

"He's always been tough," Will insisted. "Remember how he was the littlest guy on the baseball team, but he always hit the longest homers."

"Sometimes he talks like he doesn't care," Tim continued. "At first, when I went to see him in the hospital, he was full of fight. But then on the way home . . ."

"It was good that you could get your discharge so you could bring him home at least," Carrie interrupted.

18

"Well, I thought so, too, but he didn't seem that glad to see me. It's not like it was. We used to be the Three Musketeers, he and I and you, Will."

"It's my fault, isn't it?" Nancy whispered. "I wrote him about us, Tim. I had to."

"Of course you had to." Tim laid his hand over hers. "But he understood, Nancy. He even told me that he had no claim on you and he wasn't a bit jealous."

"Well, I've known Eric Arnesen for a long time," Will offered. "And he's no quitter. He lost a girl; he'll find another one. He got banged up; he'll heal."

"I sure hope so. He's my best friend, always has been and always will be." Marianne noticed how Tim's eyes caressed Nancy's sober face as he answered. "How can our happiness be complete if he can't share it?"

Chapter Three

"Tmmmn annnd," Carrie mumbled through her mouthful of straight pins.

Marianne, who stood on a kitchen chair, turned obediently as her mother pinned up the hem in the pale blue organza skirt. "Mom," she protested, "not way down to my ankles."

"It's not down to your ankles." Carrie stuck one last pin through the pleated skirt. "Though I can't figure out why Nancy wants you girls to wear short skirts for her wedding!"

Marianne giggled. "I know. In your day a bridesmaid had a bustle and a train, but times have changed. Besides, as Nancy says, she's being practical. This way we can wear our dresses to school parties later."

"Much later." Matt opened the door with a casual "Are you decent?"

"Hi, Dad." Marianne jumped down from the chair and pirouetted in front of him. "Isn't it gorgeous?"

"It's a pretty color," he admitted, "but isn't it awfully short? Next thing, you'll be wanting to show your knees."

"That's so we can wear them after the wedding, Dad."

"And just where do you plan on wearing an outfit like that at your age?"

"Daddy, I'll be a junior next year. There'll be parties, and the prom, even."

"You're only fifteen, young lady. If you think I'm going to let you go out with boys at your age—and you know how we feel about dancing."

"But I'll be sixteen then, and all the junior girls go to the prom." She turned to Carrie. "Mom, you're not going to let him treat me like a child, are you?"

Carrie smiled at Marianne. "Of course, fifteen seems very grown-up to you." She turned her smile to Matt. "And, of course, fifteen seems very young to you. I suspect we'll work something out when the time comes."

Matt lifted the lid on the cast-iron dutch oven that stood on the stove. "Smells good. When do we eat?"

"Oh, I'm sorry." Carrie reached for the soup dishes. "I guess we lost track of the time."

"It's only lunch." Matt's lips curled down, but his eyes twinkled as he teased them. "My lunch can hardly compete with Tim and Nancy's wedding after all."

"How's that new Japanese crew doing weeding the beets on the old Russell place, Matt?" Carrie asked, as she set the lunch table.

"All right, I guess. They're pretty good workers, but they could use more supervision. They've got one guy who speaks pretty good English, and I've put him in charge. I just can't stay with them all the time."

"Can't Uncle Will keep an eye on them, Dad?" Marianne asked. "That's as much his land as ours."

"He tries, but he's got his hands full on his own place."

"What about Tim?" Carrie asked. "Wasn't the Russell property supposed to be his anyhow?"

"Well, sort of. Sam and I bought it with the idea that it would be Tim's eventually. But with Anna's place to look after . . ."

"But Anna's got Uncle Eric and Harry to work her farm, Dad."

"Eric's not strong enough, Marianne," Carrie defended. "And Harry's awfully young."

"Harry's a good boy, though," Matt added. "He's got his truck garden coming along really good. He's got a dream, and I'd hate to see him discouraged from following it."

"Tim will knuckle down after the wedding, Matt," Carrie reassured him. "He can take over the new place then and still help Harry."

Matt shook his head. "It isn't just the wedding. Tim never was much for grubbing in the dirt. You know that, Carrie. And Nancy's dad's getting on in years. He's got a good dairy herd and a big investment in that creamery. I'm not surprised that Tim's spending a lot of time there and not all of it with Nancy."

"Should I call Ted and Lizzie to lunch?" Marianne interrupted. "Don't forget we're going over to Nancy's to sew this afternoon."

While their mothers were upstairs with Nancy, fitting her wedding dress, Marianne and Adele chattered away in the Johnsons' parlor and basted Nancy's going away suit. "And next year I'm going to cut my hair and curl it," Adele insisted.

"Dad would probably have a conniption fit if I bobbed my hair," Marianne muttered. "He says our bridesmaids' dresses are scandalously short."

"Men," Adele scoffed. "Well, fathers, anyhow." She sobered, then, and Marianne patted her hand. "Yeah, I know," Adele continued. "I wish Pa were here anyhow, even if he did treat me like a baby sometimes. But you know what I mean. They don't want us to grow up."

Marianne nodded. "I want to shorten my skirts, at least. But I'm not sure it's worth the bother to cut my hair."

"Even if all the other girls do?" Adele insisted. "How are we ever supposed to get husbands if we look like freaks?"

"Well, if they all do, maybe Dad won't make such a to-do. But . . ." She turned to Adele and spoke softly, so there would be no danger of her mother hearing. "George did ask me to eat with him at the picnic, even if I do still have long hair."

Adele tittered. "Everybody's jealous. He's so good looking, and on the baseball team, and captain of the debate team, and everything."

"He is nice," Marianne agreed. "I wonder if he's going up to Salinas for the rodeo next month."

"Isn't everybody?! Maybe our folks will let us go up with the other kids. The rodeo's going to be really big this year, and some of the veterans are going to put on a show too. Tim's going to play in the band, I think."

"Maybe if Dad won't let me go with George and the other kids, he'll let us go with Tim and Nancy." Marianne winked. "They'll be old married people then and can be proper chaperones."

"Hey, I never thought of that." Adele grinned. "This could be a really fun year. And, who knows, in a couple of years we could be making our own wedding dresses."

"I don't know about that," Marianne said thoughtfully. "I do want to get married and have children . . ."

"And George is such a great catch."

"Now I know you're way ahead of me," Marianne protested. "He's cute, and maybe, someday." She smiled shyly. "But I do think I want to get out on my own for a while first. Mama did, and Nancy did."

"I can't believe you're serious about being a nurse."

"Oh, but I am, Adele," Marianne insisted. "I loved the lectures on home nursing at the Chautauqua last month. I learned so much more than last year."

Adele shrugged. "If you don't want George, maybe I'll set my cap for him myself."

Marianne and Adele looked busy, basting as they talked, but they hadn't made much progress when Nancy and their mothers came back downstairs. "Are you girls going to have that suit ready for fitting soon?" Carrie asked. "We should have that done before we have to go home to fix supper."

The girls took the hint. Adele pinned pleats quietly for a while, and Marianne bit her lip as she concentrated on basting in a sleeve.

Nancy sat at the sewing machine, carefully guiding the creamy satin of her wedding dress under the needle as her foot steadily plied the treadle. Carrie and Anna sat down and each picked up a frothy bridesmaid's gown.

"Don't worry, Carrie," Anna said as she threaded her needle and began hemming Adele's dress. "It's barely the first of June, and the wedding isn't until the twenty-ninth. We've got plenty of time."

"Mom always thinks everything has to be ready weeks ahead of time," Marianne grumbled.

"Your mother's so organized." Nancy refolded the satin to start another side seam. "I wish I could be more like her."

"You'll learn," Carrie laughed. "You've had only your father to look after for a year or so. Wait until you have a husband and a couple of kids. You'll find out how important it is to be one step ahead of them."

"But you had kept house for your father and brothers for years, hadn't you, before you married Matt? And you were younger than me."

"I had to grow up a little quicker, maybe, Nancy. But you've done so much I couldn't. You've been to normal school up in San Jose. Then you went away and taught school. And when your mother died, you came home to look after your father."

"Housekeeping should be a cinch after teaching a bunch of little kids," Adele declared.

"It must be so exciting to get married and have a house of your own," Marianne mused. "But I guess you're not really going to have a house of your own, are you?"

"It is kind of funny," Nancy agreed. "I always expected to leave this house for my husband's, not have him move in here. But Pa doesn't need this big house, and he really isn't able to run the dairy by himself. Tim's a natural to take over."

Carrie and Anna looked at each other, but neither spoke. Marianne innocently voiced their concern. "But that makes it so hard for you, Gran. You have only Harry to take care of your farm and your share of the Russell place."

"Surely Eric will be able to do more soon," Nancy insisted. "Didn't you say, Anna, that he was getting better every day?"

"Oh, he is," Anna reassured them, if not herself. "He gets tired easily, but he's out in the fields every day now. We just have to be patient and keep praying."

"I do pray for him, Anna, every day." Nancy dropped her head and concentrated on her sewing.

"Is he really getting better, Anna?" Carrie inquired softly. "Matt says he's changed a lot; he's so quiet and he keeps to himself so much."

"Aunt Irene said she and Uncle Will invited him over for dinner the other night, but he wouldn't go," Marianne told them. "I guess he probably has lots of pain, because of the gas, but maybe he'd get better faster if he didn't think about it so much."

"He told me he wouldn't go because they invited Dottie Jones." Adele tittered. "He was muttering about them trying to 'fix him up.' She's cute and really nice. I can't see why he doesn't want to take her out."

"I don't think it's Dottie, girls," Carrie commented. "He's tired, and yes, Marianne, I think he is in pain too. He tries to do his share of the work, but he really needs to take it easy."

"I wish it were just his health I was worried about." Anna sighed. "But he just doesn't seem to care about anything. And he goes out a lot at night when he should be getting his sleep."

"But where?" Carrie asked. "We've asked him to come over several times, just as Will and Irene have, but he never comes."

"That night you girls mentioned—he told me he went to Will's, but he didn't."

"He lied to you!" Carrie's voice reflected her surprise. And Marianne was shocked that he would lie to his mother.

"He usually doesn't say anything at all," Anna mused.

"I thought he just went upstairs to bed early most nights," Adele said. "But Tim let it slip that he'd been out until after midnight."

"And if Tim knows where he goes, he won't tell me." Anna's voice sounded very old, Marianne realized. "You know how close they've always been, the two of them and Will. But Eric seems to avoid Tim now. Of course, Tim's out most evenings." Anna glanced at Nancy, who pedaled furiously on the treadle of her sewing machine.

Nancy seemed uncomfortable talking about Eric, Marianne thought. *It isn't her fault she loves Uncle Tim. But it's so sad that Uncle Eric can't be happy too.* And, Marianne mused, if he was staying out late at night, maybe there could be some truth in the gossip she'd heard in town. People had said Eric Arnesen had been seen on the streets of Soledad, late at night, drunk.

She hadn't dared to mention it to her mother, or even to Adele. The McLeans were all teetotalers—Salvation

Army people until the Army had given up the failed Fort Romie project, and staunch Methodists now. Uncle Eric was sick, and troubled, but he couldn't be drinking.

Marianne held out the bodice she had been basting. "I think I've got this right, Nancy. Are you ready to try it on?"

Chapter Four

*M*arianne saw the Hanlon Studebaker in the yard as she, Adele, and Harry pulled up in the truck after school. "Mom's still here," she commented. "They must not be finished with the wedding cake yet. I'll wait and ride home with her."

She caught her breath as she and Adele went into the kitchen. Gran still liked to use her old wood stove for baking, and the room was stiflingly hot.

"Hi, girls. Is it that late already?" Carrie lifted the whisk from the bowl of frothy egg whites, shook her head, and rubbed her arm. "Not quite ready," she said to Anna.

Anna measured sifted flour from a sheet of waxed paper back into the sifter. "Good. I'm not ready for them yet, either." She resifted the flour and measured it into the big enameled dishpan she was using as a mixing bowl. "I'm so proud that Nancy asked me to make her wedding cake, but now it has to live up to her expectations."

"Your baking always does, Anna," Carrie said as she continued beating the eggs. "It's going to be a perfect wedding cake and a perfect wedding."

"I just love our dresses." Adele reached for the heavy sadiron that sat on a shelf above the stove. "Shall I press mine while the cake's in the oven and the stove's good and hot?"

"Yes, do. If you get those pleats pressed in good tonight we won't have to heat up the stove in the morning," Anna agreed.

"When we get electricity next year, can we get one of those irons that heats up by itself?" Adele muttered.

Anna, who was comfortable with the old ways, ignored the question. "The dresses did turn out nice, didn't they?"

Carrie laughed. "I'm afraid Matt still doesn't approve. I guess all fathers are like that, hating to see their little girls grow up."

"Little girls! Mom, we're almost sixteen," Marianne protested.

"Sixteen. Why, when I was your age . . ."

"When I was her age, I was getting married, in Denmark, to Harold," Anna recalled.

"Don't remind Matt of that. He's still at the 'If any of those kids start hanging around here, I'll drive them off with a buggy whip' stage." Carrie handed the bowl of stiff egg whites to Anna and turned back to the girls. "Sure you're interested in boys. You wouldn't be normal if you weren't, I guess. But you've got lots of time. Enjoy your youth while you can."

30

Marianne sighed. Older people were always talking like that. *Were things really that perfect when they were in school?*

Anna folded the egg whites into her creamy cake batter and filled her own and the borrowed cake tins. She set the pans in the oven. "Be careful not to drop the iron," she warned Adele, who had begun pressing the pleats in her dress. "If that cake falls, I'll scream."

They heard the door slam. "Is that you, Eric?" Anna called. "Be careful. The wedding cake's in the oven."

"Don't worry, Ma. Your cakes never fall."

"You never see the ones that do. But the chickens have eaten a few," Anna admitted, smiling.

"Not Tim's wedding cake, anyhow," he muttered, pausing at the door. "Nothing's going to go wrong with Tim's wedding."

He went upstairs, and Anna shook her head sadly. "I'm so worried about him."

"He seems stronger, Gran," Marianne offered. "Really he does. He's breathing easier."

"Yes," Carrie concurred. "Matt tells me he's spending more time in the fields, and his color is certainly better."

"I know my son, and he's turned sullen," Anna responded. "You know Eric was always cheerful before. He liked to be out with people, doing things."

"He's been awfully sick. He gets tired. That's all, Mama." Adele tried to reassure her mother.

"It's more than that," Anna insisted. "He avoids us all. He misses meals, or if he does come to the table, he scarcely says two words. If Harry asks him something about the farm, he just grunts. Remember, Adele, how he snapped at you the other night? You were talking about something that happened at school, and he actually told you to shut up. Now that's not like Eric."

"Tim's been worried too," Carrie added. "He told me Eric insists it has nothing to do with his marrying Nancy, but, well, maybe Eric's hurting more than he wants to admit."

"Will's married, with a baby and a farm of his own. Tim's getting married and taking over the Johnson dairy. They're both healthy and prosperous, on top of the world."

"It's true, Anna. God does seem to be smiling on us all. But Eric . . ." They heard him stumble on the stairs. Anna rushed into the hallway with Carrie and Marianne at her heels. "Are you all right?" Anna called.

"Fine, Ma, just fine." He shuffled toward the front door, stuffing something in his pocket. "Sure," he muttered, "with God smiling on everybody in sight, why shouldn't I be just fine?" He was careful not to slam the door as he went out.

Marianne remembered the gossip as Anna spoke. "You smelled it, didn't you, all of you? And he had a flask in his pocket."

"Don't be silly, Anna. Eric wouldn't drink," Carrie insisted.

"He wouldn't be the only one," Anna admitted. "Lots of the boys have. They were exposed to so many things in the Army. And then to come back sick . . ."

"Eric's a Christian," Carrie protested. "The boys all took the pledge years ago."

Her mother might have heard the gossip, too, Marianne realized. "Maybe it's just his medicine," she said softly.

"Maybe." Anna looked down at her knotted hands. "I think he's taking morphine for the pain. But could that change him so much? He's so alone, and he won't let us help him."

"Maybe he will when the wedding is over," Carrie offered. "Maybe when things get back to normal, and he's stronger."

A cool sea breeze brought a refreshing morning mist to the Fort Romie community on Tim and Nancy's wedding day. Marianne and Liz were up at dawn and outside cutting the choicest blossoms from the wild roses that bloomed around the house. Marianne had climbed high on a ladder, reaching for the clusters of pink that clung to the eaves and dropping them into the basket Liz held, when their mother called them in for breakfast.

"Liz, go out to the barn and tell your father and Ted that breakfast is ready. Marianne, you can help me put it on the table."

"I couldn't eat a mouthful, Mom." Marianne brushed rose petals from her auburn hair as she bounced into the kitchen. "I'm much too excited. And we have so much to do."

"After we all have a good breakfast," Carrie insisted.

"But we have to decorate the church, and then we have to go to Nancy's house and get dressed and help her get dressed."

"And, and, and." Carrie laughed. "Have you got enough flowers?"

"Probably not, but Adele's bringing some from their house, and there are lots over by the mission ruins. We can go over and get some of those before we go to the church."

"Sounds like you have everything under control, then," her mother assured her. "So you have plenty of time for breakfast."

Plenty of time or not, the two girls were off at top speed a few minutes later, flower baskets swinging as they skipped down the dusty lane. "I'll meet you at the church in an hour or so," Carrie called after them.

By the time Carrie got to the church, Marianne and Adele had made bouquets of the fresh pink and white roses, tied them with white satin ribbon bows, and tacked them to the pews flanking the center aisle. "I found some wild daisies over at the mission, too," Marianne explained to her mother, as she arranged the best of the roses, daisies, and feathery wild grasses in a large vase.

"It looks beautiful," Carrie told them. She took the vase from Marianne and set it on the piano as Adele set flower-filled white baskets on either side of the simple altar. "I do believe we're finished. Where are the flowers for your bouquets?"

"I left them in the shade down by the creek to keep cool," Marianne told her. "Do you really think the church looks nice, Mom?"

"I think it looks perfect. Are you ready to go to Nancy's?"

All of the little community of Fort Romie and half of Soledad turned out to share in the wedding celebration. Even the weather cooperated. The wind remained light, and the fog burned off just in time for the kind of warm summer afternoon the valley was famous for.

Marianne had been afraid she'd trip and spoil everything as she walked down the aisle in her first high heels, but she didn't have any trouble. Her Uncle Will, as best man, stood to one side of the altar with his brother. Harry was up there, too, looking absolutely absurd, Marianne thought, in his high, starched collar and black suit. Tim had also asked Eric to stand up with him, she knew, but Eric had said he didn't feel well enough.

Marianne took her place opposite the men and turned to wait for Adele to join her. Then all eyes turned to Nancy as she started down the aisle in her beautiful satin gown. *Will I be next?* Marianne wondered. George did seem awfully interested. *But Mom's right. I've got lots of time. What's the big hurry to get married, just so you can keep house and have babies? Not that I don't want babies, but not yet.*

After the ceremony, the wedding cake and fruit punch had been served in the picnic grounds across the lane from the church. Now the family was gathering the scattered plates and cups. It had been a perfect wedding, Marianne thought. Eric's words might have been spoken in bitterness, but they had come true anyhow. *Eric?* "Where's Uncle Eric?" she said aloud.

"I haven't seen him since the ceremony," Adele answered. "Mama, where's Eric?"

35

Anna frowned. "I wish I knew. He left right after we cut the cake, and I haven't seen him since."

"He was probably tired and just went home," Marianne suggested. "He looked like he felt really sick earlier."

"I thought he was with Will and Harry, getting the car fixed up," Matt commented. "But they came back long before Tim and Nancy were ready to leave on their honeymoon. Harry," he called, "was Eric with you earlier?"

"No, Matt. We asked him to help us with the car, but he said he didn't feel too well and was going home."

Will joined them, tossing a bottle into the paper bag he was using for trash. "Punch wasn't good enough for somebody, I guess." He shrugged. "What's everybody looking so glum about?"

"We were wondering what happened to Eric," Anna explained.

Marianne picked up a heavy box of dirty plates, handed it to Adele, and picked up another. "Gran, we'll take these back to your house to wash them. We can make sure Uncle Eric's all right."

Eric was sitting on the porch steps, chin in his hands, staring blankly out across Harry's thriving lettuce patch when the girls came up.

"Mama's worried about you," Adele told him.

"Tough," he grunted. "Why doesn't she just forget about me, like everyone else?"

"Nobody's forgetting about you," Adele snapped. "They're all wondering why you ran off like that. You didn't even stay to see Tim and Nancy off on their honeymoon."

"I didn't feel like it."

"You shouldn't worry Mama so," Adele persisted.

"Oh, quit your nagging. Just leave me alone!"

Marianne felt tears welling up in her eyes. "Uncle Eric, can I help? Would you like me to get you some of your medicine or something?"

"No!" He answered so sharply that the tears in her eyes brimmed over.

"I just wanted to help," she said softly. "Come on, Adele. Let's get started on these dishes."

Adele took her apron from its hook and tossed her mother's to Marianne. "Mama won't mind if you use this. We sure don't want to spoil our dresses."

They'd just started heating the dishwater when Eric stumbled into the kitchen. "I'm sorry, kids. I feel all worn out. But I shouldn't have taken it out on you."

Adele just shrugged, but Marianne turned to him and smiled. "We knew you weren't mad at us," she told him. "I'm sorry you feel so bad."

He looked at her and seemed oddly puzzled, like he wasn't sure who she was. Marianne could smell alcohol on his breath. *I guess he's drunk,* she thought, but she'd never been around people who drank. "Uncle Eric, shouldn't you maybe go upstairs and lie down if you're not feeling well?"

"I'm all right," he insisted, though he obviously wasn't. "I'll help."

He picked up the teakettle, but his hand shook so much that the scalding water spilled on the floor. Adele reached out to take the kettle from him. "I'm not an invalid," he mumbled. "I said I'd help with the dishes."

"You can't. See, you're spilling the water," Adele protested.

He shoved her roughly. "Get out of here. You and Mama, fussing, always fussing. Get out of the way."

Both girls shrank back, frightened. He pointed to Marianne, and his voice was slurred. "You, you can stay. You're nice."

"He really shouldn't be alone," Marianne whispered to Adele. "Maybe you should go get your mother, or maybe my dad or Will."

"Are you sure?" Adele's chin trembled. "I've never seen him like this. I'm afraid."

"Well, I'm not," Marianne lied. "We can't leave him alone, and he needs help. Go on," she insisted.

"You're nice," Eric said again to Marianne. "Tell her to go back to Mama and leave me alone."

Adele looked at Marianne again, and Marianne nodded. Adele backed out of the kitchen.

Marianne's hand quivered as she filled the dishpan. She wasn't sure what she was afraid of. At the Chautauqua, they had said that morphine made people act strangely, and Uncle Eric's behavior certainly wasn't normal.

She washed the delicate translucent plates and stood them carefully in the rubber draining rack. Eric dried several and put them up on the top shelf. Then one dropped from his hands to the pine floor.

"Oh," Marianne gasped. "Gran's best china!"

"So what? So now I'm not good enough even to dry dishes?"

"I didn't mean that, Uncle Eric. It was an accident." He was glaring at her. His cheeks flamed red against his ashen gray skin, and his breathing, though shallow, was very fast. Marianne's vague uneasiness became terror, not for herself, but for her uncle. "Please, Uncle Eric, it isn't important. Come sit down in the parlor for a while and rest."

"No, outside, where it's cooler," he gasped, accepting her offered arm and walking with her to the porch steps.

He dropped down on the steps again, hiding his face in his trembling hands. Marianne hoped Anna would be back soon. "Nancy," she heard him mutter, as he stood on shaky legs, "Got to see Nancy."

"No, don't," she protested. "Uncle Eric, Nancy isn't home. Don't you remember? She got married today, to Uncle Tim."

"Nancy's my girl." He frowned, as if puzzled by her words. "Nancy's my girl, and Tim's my best friend."

Marianne followed him as he shuffled down the road. She caught up and took his arm as he stumbled. *Why, oh why wasn't Adele back by now with help?*

The had reached the ruins of Mission Soledad when he suddenly dragged her behind an old adobe wall. She was too stunned, for an instant, to resist. And in that instant he pushed her to the ground, pinning her with the weight of his body. What happened next she would never remember clearly, nor ever completely forget.

Chapter Five

Marianne was only dimly aware of the twilight shadows. She huddled, shivering despite the June warmth, hidden among the ruins of the old Spanish Soledad Mission. Her fingers fumbled and tried to retie Gran's big apron. Under it, her first grown-up party dress was crumpled and torn. The bow that had held her hair in a knot of curls lay on the ground beside her; the curls dangled around her trembling shoulders.

Her thoughts were a disjointed jumble. She couldn't go home looking like she did: dress awry, hair straggly. And she couldn't go home feeling like she did: dirty, violated, terrified. She wanted a hot bath, scalding hot, and strong lye soap to scrub away the evil thing she knew wouldn't go away, ever, with any amount of washing.

Marianne Hanlon, fifteen years old, lived in a world where such things didn't happen, and even if they did, Matt and Carrie would never let them happen to her. Yesterday she'd never even heard of such a horror. Gossip, perhaps, about things terrible men did to sinful women who "led them on," but Uncle Eric . . .

The moon was coming up, and Marianne had to go home. There was no place else for a fifteen-year-old girl to go. But she mustn't let them know what happened. If they knew, her life would be ended before it had begun. There would be no school parties, no nurse's training, no beaus and never, ever a wedding of her own. No decent person would have anything to do with her ever again. Her world had taught her that such things didn't happen to good girls.

Marianne managed, somehow, to smooth the wrinkled dress and cover the tears with Anna's apron. She tied her curls back and washed her face in the old mission well. Maybe she could sneak into the house and upstairs to her room without being seen. Maybe Liz, who shared her room, wouldn't notice. Maybe by tomorrow some of the horror would fade.

But as she reached the lane, she saw her father. "Marianne, where on earth have you been?" he demanded. "Adele told us Eric was acting strangely, but when we got back to the house there was no one there. Your mother is worried sick."

"I, I'm sorry, Daddy." She fought to sound calm. *I can't tell them. I can't. But I have to tell them something.* "Uncle Eric," she whispered. "Uncle Eric wandered away, and I was so worried about him."

"Adele thought he'd been drinking."

"I guess so," Marianne agreed. "He said something about going to see Nancy, and that scared me."

"Nancy?"

"Yes, Daddy. He wasn't making sense. So I came to look for him, but I didn't find him." She wasn't in the habit of lying, and the words did not come easily.

"Then why didn't you come back to Anna's, or go on home? It's been over an hour since Adele came and got us."

An hour. Only an hour, she thought. "An hour, Daddy? I didn't realize it had been that long. I, I thought he might have gone over to the mission. You know, it's a nice place to be alone. He said he wanted to be alone, Daddy, but I knew he was sick, and I didn't think he should be alone."

"Well, you meant well, I guess," her father chided. "But next time make sure we know where you are. You've no idea the things that can happen to a little girl out by herself."

"Oh, thank God you've found her." Carrie rushed up, breathless. "Marianne, you shouldn't have stayed out so late. We were worried about you."

"Eric wandered off, and she was worried about him. She went looking for him."

"Oh, good. Is he all right? Anna's frantic."

"I, I didn't find him, Mama."

"Well, thank God you're safe, anyhow."

Her mother seemed to accept the explanation. Marianne was grateful for the darkness. Surely they would know something was very wrong if they could see her face. She said nothing until they reached the Hanlon farm house and wearily climbed the porch steps. "Mama, I'm awfully tired. Is it all right if I go right upstairs to bed?"

Marianne heard Lizzie and Ted chattering downstairs and hoped Carrie wouldn't send them to bed too soon. She pulled the quilt up over her head, so that Liz would think she was already asleep.

She trembled, remembering. Uncle Eric had been so sad and lonely. *I only tried to be nice to him,* she thought. *I was trying to cheer him up.* "Oh, God," Marianne prayed. "Oh God, don't let me remember."

But it was as if she had to live the awful minutes over and over again, feel again the sudden, rough, hungry embrace, endure being dragged behind the crumbling adobe walls of the mission, feel herself thrown down on the hard, bare ground.

She wondered how, sick as he was, he had had the strength to overpower her. He must have been driven by some insane rage. She remembered how heavy he had felt as she had struggled. It had seemed he would crush the life out of her. "I wish he had," she sobbed into her pillow. Her throat still burned from the screams she'd screamed where no one could hear. And her body ached from the struggle, and from the thing he had done to her.

She heard Liz come into their room and kept her face buried in her pillow until her sister had blown out the kerosene lamp. Why, oh why had he done such a thing to her? She searched her memory desperately. *What did I ever do to make him do it? Oh, God,* she prayed in the frightful stillness. *Oh, God, if you will still hear me, what did I do wrong? Why did he do that to me? Why did you let him hurt me that way?*

God did hear, despite her fears, and in his mercy let her fall into an exhausted sleep. Once she woke herself,

43

screaming in her dreams, but Liz drowsily accepted her excuse, "Just a nightmare."

She awoke very early in the morning to the ugly memory and to the one question she had to answer. How could she face her mother? Carrie would certainly know, the moment she saw her, that Marianne had a terrible secret.

She kept the quilt over her head as Liz got up, dressed, and went downstairs. But Liz was back up the stairs almost immediately. "Marianne, Marianne, you sleepyhead." She pulled back the quilt and shook her sister none-too-gently. "Marianne, you have to get up and come downstairs right away. Something awful's happened, and Mama and Anna want to talk to you."

They know already! No, Marianne told herself. *That is impossible.* "What?" she snapped. "What's happened that they want to talk to me about?"

"It's something about Uncle Eric," Liz told her, "and you don't have to bite my head off. Mama said to get you right away because you saw him after the rest of us did."

Marianne stumbled through the mechanics of washing her face, dressing, combing her hair. *They couldn't know*, she told herself. *Surely he wouldn't have told anyone.* She glanced in the wall mirror and tried to convince herself that she still looked as she had yesterday. But somehow, she was sure, this evil that had changed her forever inside must show itself outside too.

She crept downstairs. Anna was waiting in the hall. "Marianne." Her voice was fearful, pleading. "Marianne, when you saw Eric yesterday afternoon after the wedding, did he say anything about where he was going, anything at all?"

They don't know, Marianne realized. Thank God for that, but then, what was Anna asking her? She tried to focus her numbed mind on the question and the answer she had to give. "No," she said at first, not wanting to worry Anna more. "Well, yes." She corrected herself hesitantly. "But it didn't really make sense. He said he was going to see Nancy."

Anna looked pained. "Nancy?"

Marianne didn't want to talk to anyone about anything, but she especially didn't want to talk about Eric. "I know it doesn't make sense. He was confused. He didn't seem to know what he was saying. That's why I sent Adele to get you, and why I went with him—followed him," she corrected quickly, remembering the story she'd told the night before.

Anna didn't seem to notice the slip. "I'm very worried about him, Marianne. He never came home last night."

Marianne was afraid her relief showed. *Thank God I don't have to face him again, not right away anyhow,* she thought, as Anna continued.

"I found a note this morning, and it's so scary."

Carrie joined them at the foot of the stairs, and Marianne saw that she had an envelope in her hand. "Come into the sitting room. Maybe you'll remember something he said that will help Anna understand or help us find him."

"He was sad about the wedding." Marianne still struggled to keep her voice from betraying her secret, but she realized her mother's and grandmother's thoughts were focused only on Eric and his disappearance. "I guess he felt worse about Tim and Nancy getting married than he wanted to let on."

"But he didn't say anything to you about going away?" Anna pressed.

"No, he didn't." She remembered some of Eric's incoherent rambling. "He talked about being sick, mostly, and about the war. He said he'd gone off to fight for his country and now he'd lost his health, and his girl, and his best friend." She bit her lip and struggled to hold back her tears. "He seemed to hate everybody," she said. *And he must have hated me, too,* she thought, *but why? And now I hate him, and I can't even tell them that I hate him.*

"I knew he was bitter," his mother said. "I tried to make him talk about it, so I could help him get rid of it, but he kept insisting it was only the gassing and the pain."

"Yes," Carrie agreed. "We knew he was troubled, but the note doesn't sound bitter, just so terribly sad."

"Note?" Marianne asked.

"I found a note in his room this morning," Anna explained.

Carrie held the envelope out to her daughter, but Marianne couldn't bring herself to touch it. She blinked back tears, and Carrie opened the envelope and read the brief note. "You're the best thing in my life, Mother, and now I've hurt you and those you love, and I can never forgive myself. I know you can never forgive me either, and I just can't stay here and face you all. Don't worry about me; I'm not worth it."

If he'd asked forgiveness, she could never have given it, but now, despite her own anguish, Marianne's tears were for him as much as for herself.

"Why did he think he'd hurt us?" Anna asked. "We knew he was sick. We didn't expect him to work as hard as he used to. We loved him; we wanted to help him."

Carrie faced Anna and reached out, taking the older woman's hands in her slender ones. "Anna, you knew Eric had been drinking, didn't you?"

"You knew too? You denied it day before yesterday, when he came in while the cake was in the oven."

"Matt and I had both heard gossip in town, but I didn't want to believe it. Anna, it must have been the pain. They gave him morphine, I guess, in the hospital, and maybe he was still taking that, too, but he was in a lot of pain."

"I do know that, Carrie, and I understood. Surely he knew I could understand that. Marianne." She turned to the sobbing teenager. "When she came for us, Adele said he was acting strangely. He was drunk, wasn't he?"

"I, I think so," she nodded. "I tried to cheer him up. I only tried to cheer him up." Marianne knew she could control her words no longer. She turned and fled, carrying her secret with her. From the stairs she heard Anna's tender words. "She's such a dear, sensitive child, Carrie."

I must never tell them, the girl vowed silently. *It would break Gran's heart if she ever found out.*

Chapter Six

*S*top! No! Please, no!" Marianne's cries woke her and her sister to the stillness of the night. She shook with the fear that stayed, always, at best, just beneath her consciousness.

"Another nightmare, sis?" Liz asked sleepily. "Maybe you should tell Mom about them."

"I'm not going to bother Mom about a few bad dreams, Liz. And don't you, either. She's got enough to worry about, helping Dad and the boys with all the farm work, and trying to cheer Anna up, and helping Irene and Nancy with their canning, and everything."

"But you never used to have nightmares, Marianne. Now you've had them almost every night for a couple of weeks, ever since the wedding."

"I'm sorry, Liz. But I'm sure they'll stop soon. Go back to sleep." Marianne lay still in her bed, trying to concentrate on something, anything—anything to keep from falling asleep again and dreaming again.

Oh, God. She sighed as she stared at the sloping ceiling and tried to pray silently. *Oh, please, dear God forgive me and help me to forgive him.* Marianne had never really understood what the preacher meant when he talked about fornication, but she knew what had happened was evil. *God, I didn't mean for it to happen,* she pleaded. *Please, please, dear Jesus, don't let Mama find out, or Gran, or Dad—especially not Dad.*

Marianne adored her father, but she feared him, too, and he was always warning her about boys and what nasty things they might do to her if she gave them any opportunity. *I didn't lead him on,* she told herself. *But I must have. I must have done something wrong, or it wouldn't have happened.*

But when she tried to figure out where she had gone astray, she had to force herself to remember the twilight walk. Yes, Eric had been angry. He had said awful things about Uncle Tim, and about Nancy too. He'd said that Nancy had betrayed him. "You'd never do that, Marianne," he had said to her.

But then he'd seemed confused. *It must have been the whisky,* she concluded. He'd muttered something about Nancy's honeymoon, but then, as he had dragged her back behind the mission walls, he had called her Nancy. *That must have been it. He wanted to hurt Nancy, but he was drunk and confused.*

"Please, dear Jesus," she whispered into her pillow, "please show me what I did wrong and forgive me. Please heal the hurt, and help me to forgive him."

When Marianne woke again, the sun was streaming in her window and her mother was standing in the

49

doorway. "Marianne, honey, you'd better get up if you're going to Salinas for the rodeo today."

"You're only fifteen," her father had said when she had proposed the trip. "I don't think you should go all the way to Salinas with a bunch of kids."

Marianne was almost thankful for his reluctance, but Adele, who suspected her own permission depended on Marianne's, protested. "Tim and Nancy said they'd chaperone, and you know all the kids. Joanie Pelham's only fourteen, and her parents are letting her go."

"If George were Marianne's brother I'd feel better about letting her go too," Matt explained with a grin. "Besides, Tim's going to be busy playing in the new American Legion Band. He won't have time to look after you kids."

"Harry's going. Mama even said he could take our truck," Adele reminded him.

"But Harry's a boy, and he's older. Anna hasn't said yet that you could go, has she?"

"She said I could go if Marianne did."

"Matt," Carrie intervened. "We do know everyone who's going, and I think we can trust Tim and Nancy to keep an eye on things."

"But they won't all fit in Tim's flivver." Matt looked at Carrie, and then at the two girls. "Oh, all right, but you two ride with Tim and Nancy, and no pairing off in the rumble seat. Understand?"

Her father repeated the warning that Saturday morning when Harry pulled the McLean truck into the yard. "See that you're all home by dark," he warned.

He needn't worry, Marianne thought, as she wedged into the seat beside Adele. *Not about George, or the other Fort Romie kids, anyhow.*

"Lucy Banister's going with us," Adele whispered to Marianne. "And Harry's sweet on her, so we're supposed to ride in back and get her to sit next to him. Okay?"

"Sure," Marianne agreed. "But why doesn't he just drop us at Tim and Nancy's first? Daddy said we have to ride with them."

"Oh, don't be silly, Marianne. That wouldn't be any fun. We're all going in the truck, you and me and Joanie and the boys too."

"But Dad said . . ."

"What he doesn't know won't hurt us. Besides, we *are* going with Tim and Nancy. They'll be right behind us on the road. What could possibly happen, except that we might have a little fun?"

Marianne wanted to have fun. She'd never been to the Salinas Rodeo before, and she wasn't going to be a spoilsport. After all, Adele was right. *What could possibly happen?* But a tiny voice inside her whispered doubts. *And what could possibly happen when you were with your own uncle?*

They arrived at what had been the Johnson place, where the newlyweds had set up housekeeping. Their friends had all gathered there, and Tim's rumble seat was already occupied by an older neighbor, another member of the American Legion band, and his great big tuba. There was nothing to do, Marianne saw, but to curl up in a corner of the truck bed.

George chose the place next to her, but he didn't seem to notice as she rearranged the bulging picnic hamper so it sat between them. The others hadn't a care in the world, Marianne thought. They gossiped about last year's triumphs and next year's prospects.

"Next year you'll lick that Salinas High debate team good," Adele assured George, after Ernie had reminded him of last year's debacle.

"Oh, sure," he grunted. "Did that Johnnie Steinbeck graduate? I might have a chance if he did."

"They're getting the baseball league going again," said Joanie. "Are you going to play, Bill?"

It wasn't fair, Marianne told herself. They were all so wrapped up in such unimportant things. Marianne had been raised in a world where life wasn't fair to everyone, but her own world, up to now, had been safe, clean, and secure.

Someone started a song, and Marianne tried to sing along with the others as the truck bounced along behind Tim's Model T.

Midway between the Gavilan Range to the east and the Santa Lucia Mountains to the west, Salinas City had grown up where the Salinas River and its rich valley made a broad curve westward toward the ocean. When the railroad came, Salinas won the roundhouse and yards, and with that, it had become the county seat and business center of the region.

The rodeo had started back in 1913 and had been the biggest event of the summer the past few years, but it was a long drive from Soledad. Matt and Carrie had talked of going sometime, but the farm work always seemed more important, so Marianne had never taken part in the festivities.

There was a parade that morning, but they arrived too late to see it. Harry drove the back streets through the town, past its handful of stylish Victorian mansions and its hundreds of simple frame cottages. The dusty fields surrounding the Rodeo grounds were full of Model Ts, most with truck conversions, and an occasional Studebaker or brand-new Chevy. Not many Salinas people had REOs or Packards.

The Rodeo grounds themselves were festooned with flags and red, white, and blue bunting. Surrounding the jerry-built grandstands were booths built of scrap lumber, gaily decorated with Japanese lanterns. The aroma of sausages came from some, gingerbread and fudge from others.

Little boys in knickers and girls in knee-high cotton stockings squealed with delight. Some of their mothers still wore heavy serge skirts that reached down to their ankles, and heavy braids wrapped around their heads. But styles were changing fast. Marianne and Adele still wore middy blouses, but their pleated skirts were slim and stopped a few inches below their knees. Despite her father's reluctance, Marianne's auburn braids had been replaced by short, bouncy curls that George had pronounced "Swell."

Local ranchers' sons competed with cowboys from as far away as Sacramento and Los Angeles. They showed off the roping and riding skills that were still used every day in the valley, and the girls jumped up and down and cheered for their favorites. When a Soledad cowboy succeeded in riding an especially mean bronco, George circled Marianne's waist with his arm. She stiffened, despite her excitement. She managed to stifle a cry and felt relieved when George whispered an embarrassed "sorry" and dropped his arm.

"Hey, kids," Tim called through the cheering crowd as the winning riders threw hats in the air and claimed their prizes. "We'd better get going if we're going to make it home before dark."

"Aw, can't we stay for the fireworks?" Adele protested.

"Matt'll have my head as it is." Tim grinned as he shooed them toward the parking area.

Marianne was astonished when Harry checked his father's old pocketwatch and told them it was nearly six o'clock. The day had gone so quickly, and it really had been fun, she realized. Maybe she could forget, sometime, as long as nobody else knew.

They piled into the truck. None of them got to Salinas more than once or twice a year, and they eagerly pointed out the sights as they chugged through the town that, with 4,000 people, looked like a metropolis to them. The big new high school made the one they went to in Gonzales look tawdry. "And there's going to be a college this fall," George bragged. "Only two years, but still, a college just up the road from us, less than forty miles away. I sure would like to go there."

"They have a nursing school at the hospital," Marianne mused. *But,* she thought, *they'd never accept me if they knew.* She wriggled into the far corner of the truck bed, as far away from the happy group as she could move.

As they passed the sprawling Spreckles Sugar Mill south of the town, someone started a song. Marianne tried to hum along, but the memories had come back.

The singing continued as the miles of farmland passed and twilight fell. She thought of moving closer to Adele, but Adele had deftly settled herself between George and Ernie.

By the time they passed Gonzales High School, the moon had risen over the Gavilan Mountains. Joanie looked like she'd fallen asleep. Bill, whose fine bass had been leading the singing, began a lovely new ballad by Sigmund Romberg. "I'm falling in love with someone," he crooned. George caught Marianne's eye and smiled at her as he joined in the song. She should have been so happy, but she shivered in the evening breeze and stared out across the dark valley.

The nightmares persisted, but Marianne couldn't tell her mother about them. Her refusal was rooted in her fear of revealing what had happened the evening of Tim's wedding. Still, the excuse she gave her sister was true too. Summer on the farm left little free time for fretting about anything. They all stayed so busy that Marianne could even push her hurt aside for hours at a time.

The three generations of women often gathered in Carrie's big, modern kitchen. Working together made the chores go faster, Carrie and Anna told each other. Nancy, more at home in a schoolroom than a kitchen, joined them, eager to learn the homemaking skills that had become second nature to the older women. Adele was a less willing pupil, and last year she and Marianne had schemed, finding all kinds of excuses to avoid the endless pickling and preserving.

But this summer Marianne welcomed the hard work and the company. Sitting at the old oak table opposite Adele, cutting juicy corn from the cob, she could still be a little girl.

"You are going to the baseball game Sunday afternoon, aren't you?" Adele was saying. "Joanie said George told her he wanted to sit with you."

"I guess I'll go." Marianne shrugged. "Harry's pitching, isn't he?"

"Yeah, I guess so. Who cares?"

"Adele, you should be ashamed," Anna scolded. "Your brother's the star of the team."

"But he's my *brother*." Adele made it sound like he was a leper or worse. "I do wish he'd introduce me to that handsome new shortstop, though."

"I don't," her mother retorted. "He's much too old for you."

Adele leaned across the table and whispered to Marianne. "They think we're such children. Why, in a couple more years we'll be through high school. If we just wait around, the good men will all be taken."

She giggled and glanced toward her mother, who was stirring the relish on the gas stove. "I think George is the nicest boy in the whole school, Marianne. Are you going to sit with him at the ball game? Because if you're not, I'm going to get him for myself."

"Go ahead." Marianne applied herself to the pan of corn on the table. "If you want him, he's all yours."

"Come on, Marianne," Adele coaxed. "If you're not interested in George, who do you have your eye on? Bill? Ernie?"

"Nobody," Marianne snapped. "Can't you talk about anything but boys?"

"Well, I'm sooo sorry. What's the matter with you, anyhow?"

"Nothing." Marianne saw her mother's frown. "I'm sorry, Adele. I didn't mean to snap at you. I guess I'm just hot and tired."

"Sure. There must be better ways to spend an afternoon than making corn relish." Adele idly sawed a row of corn from the cob. "Must have been some way we could have gotten out of this," she whispered.

Marianne thought of how easily she could have avoided the relish making. If Mom had known how she was feeling, she'd have given her a dose of peppermint and sent her to bed. *But I can't stay in my room alone, thinking,* Marianne had told herself when the waves of nausea came as she awoke. *It's just nerves, and it only gets worse when I think about it. No, I have to keep busy, even if it means listening to Adele's incessant chatter.* "Maybe," she whispered back. "But what have we got to do that's any better?"

Adele shrugged. "I guess I'll be glad when school starts. There'll be lots of fun then—picnics and square dances and hayrides."

"And classes," Carrie reminded the girls.

"And classes," Marianne agreed. "I think chemistry's going to be really interesting."

"Chemistry? Are you crazy? Nobody likes chemistry," Adele insisted.

"Why not? Besides, I have to understand science if I'm going to be a nurse. That's a lot more important than parties and boyfriends." Marianne bent her head over her work. *I'll be a good nurse*, she told herself. *That's all I want to be.*

Adele shook her head. "I sure don't know what's happened to you. You're no fun at all anymore."

Marianne felt sick again on Sunday, but she didn't want her mother to worry, so she struggled through the morning sermon without hearing it and joined the rest of the family at the baseball game that was the highlight of their simple social life.

Later, as they cleared the table after their supper, Carrie made an unusual offer to her younger daughter. "You can go play for a while, Liz," she suggested. "I'll help Marianne with the dishes."

"How come Liz gets off and not me?" Marianne grumbled.

"Oh, I wanted to have a little girl-to-girl chat with you, that's all." She put a stack of dishes in the sink and reached for the steaming teakettle.

Marianne did not feel like chatting. She had felt miserable all day although she decided she would have been even more miserable if she had stayed home alone.

Eric had been gone for nearly two months, but whenever Marianne was alone, it seemed she could feel his presence—his shuffling footsteps, his hacking cough, his husky voice. "Marianne, you're such a pretty girl," he had said. "And you'd never lead a guy on and then dump him for his best friend, would you?"

When she was alone she remembered and walked with him past the old mission again. *For a while he talked to me like I was grown up,* she thought. *And I tried to be nice to him. And then he* . . . So she had gone to the game, to keep from being alone.

"Marianne." Her mother's voice broke through her thoughts. "Marianne, what's wrong with you?"

"What do you mean, Mama? Nothing's wrong," she replied.

"You were a million miles away." Carrie smiled as she handed her daughter a dish towel. "Come back. Or are your daydreams that much better than a talk with your mother?"

My daydreams. My daydreams are all nightmares anymore, Marianne thought. "Of course, I'd rather talk with my mother, but why do I think this is going to be a lecture?"

"Oh, no. I do hope I'm not becoming one of 'those' mothers. No, it's just that you seem awfully preoccupied lately. And, well, this afternoon you were really rather rude to George. Has he done anything to offend you, Marianne?"

"No, Mom. George is all right, but . . ."

"He seems like a nice boy, Marianne, but if he's been annoying you, you would tell me, wouldn't you?"

If only it were George, the girl thought. *If it were George I'd tell her, and Dad, and* . . . Besides, the thought of George doing to her what Eric had done was almost laughable, if Marianne could still laugh. *George! That child*. "Mom, George hasn't 'annoyed' me, as you put it. I just didn't feel like sitting with him today."

"Nor like going berrying with the other kids tomorrow?"

"I said I'd help you with the laundry. I promised to help you this summer, and the summer is nearly over."

"Summer is nearly over, and while I appreciate your help, I think I could have spared you. Marianne, when I was your age, I didn't have much chance for fun. My mother had died, and I had the boys to look after. I wasn't much older than you when I went to work at the Emporium."

"I know, Mom." The chat was beginning to sound a little like a lecture after all.

"Marianne," Carrie continued, "I want you to have fun. And besides, we'd all enjoy the blackberries, so why don't you call Adele and tell her you'll go with them after all?"

The wild blackberry bushes grew along the irrigation ditches that crisscrossed the valley farms. Between the muddy channels, sugar beets formed green ripples, and the swaying wheat was beginning to turn to gold. The hills were brown in the distance, but in the fertile valley it was nearly harvest time.

The best berries grew closest to the ditches, and the three lanky boys had struggled through the thorny thicket. Marianne, Adele, and Joanie strolled along the upper edge, reaching out now and then to pluck a nearby berry.

True to her promise, Adele set her pace to match George's. He seemed to be enjoying her attention, Marianne thought.

He stretched up to give a full pail to Adele, who fluttered her blonde lashes as she handed down an empty one. "You certainly do know where to find the best berries," Adele gushed. "Why, I haven't filled one pail yet."

"They're down here where it's wet." Adele peered over the hedge, as if considering joining him. "Oh, no, Adele," George protested. "You'd get scratched and spoil your dress. You just stay up there, and I'll pick plenty for you."

"George really likes you better," Joanie confided to Marianne. "Why are you mad at him?"

"I'm not mad at him," she replied absently. "George is okay."

"Then why did you tell him to go away yesterday?" Joanie persisted. "You really hurt his feelings."

"Then I'm sorry." Marianne's voice was sharper than she intended.

"Oh, Marianne, you're so cross all the time lately." Joanie scrambled through a thin patch in the thicket and joined Bill, the youngest of the boys. Taking her cue from the flirtatious Adele, she cooed coyly, "I thought the picking would be better down here."

Marianne picked idly, scarcely noticing the casual pairing. She felt nauseated again and wondered if she should tell her mother. *No,* she decided once again. *There's no reason to worry her. It's just because I'm not sleeping well. It's the nightmares and remembering. I've got to learn not to remember.*

"Marianne." She jumped as Ernie called to her. "Hey, wake up," he teased. "Can you give me a hand with this bucket?"

She leaned across the tangled bushes and took the pail, heavy with its rich purple harvest. Then as she started to give him the last empty one, her foot slipped on the damp adobe soil, and she tumbled, head first, into the blackberry patch.

As she fell, she heard laughter from her friends. *Well, I probably do look funny,* she realized, *with my head in the bushes and my feet kicking up behind me.* The thorns ripping her cheeks were not funny, though.

"Ouch," she heard Adele's sympathetic moan. "Marianne, hold still and let us get you loose. You won't get scratched up as much."

She saw Ernie's berry-stained fingers reach for her arm. Her sleeve was snagged on dozens of the long spines, and he tore it away to free her. As his fingers brushed her shoulder, she recoiled. "Stop it," she screamed. "Don't touch me! Don't touch me!"

The boy drew back, startled. Marianne was shaking, violently, still screaming for him to get away from her. "Gosh, Marianne, I didn't mean anything." He turned a beet-red face to Adele and the others. "Gosh, I didn't mean anything. I was just trying to help her get loose."

Chapter Seven

*M*arianne started school with iodine-painted scratches on her pert nose and rosy cheeks, but she knew those would soon heal. The nightmares came much less often, and even the annoying nausea that had persisted all summer had finally disappeared. The deep cuts remained, inside, but Marianne was young. She was sure of her parents' love and of God's love, and the raw, festering hurt was slowly scarring over.

With September came school and the hot, dry east winds that signaled the wheat harvest. The sugar beets were dug and piled high along the railroad tracks, loaded onto almost endless freight cars and hauled up to the mill in Salinas.

Harry McLean harvested the last of his cabbages and carrots quickly, lest they go to seed in the sudden heat, and took them to San Francisco where they sold readily at the produce market. He had been right. His vegetables, grown in the cool coastal valley, had brought good prices all summer.

Eric Arnesen had not returned to the valley, for which Marianne thanked God every morning. She knew, though, that Anna was praying just as fervently that he would return, or at least write and let her know he was safe.

Marianne and Adele shared families, friends, and classmates, and they also shared birthdays. They had actually been born a week apart, but they had always celebrated together.

"And we'll be sixteen," Adele was saying. "Surely Mama and your mother will let us have a real party this year." The two girls were walking home from the Pelham farm after school, since George was driving the informal "school bus" to Gonzales now. "And I don't mean a bunch of girls on Saturday afternoon. I mean a real party, with boys, at night."

"Dad would never let us have dancing, Adele." Marianne didn't say so to Adele, but she was very grateful that he wouldn't. They were walking past the old mission, and she shivered at the memories and the thought of any boy putting his arm around her. "Dad doesn't believe in dancing."

"Why not? Mama thinks it's all right, as long as there's a chaperone, of course. What's going to happen?"

"Maybe something terrible. You know—boys get ideas. Dad says so, and so does the preacher."

"That's so old fashioned," Adele insisted. "We'd only have boys we knew, like George and Ernie and Bill. Can you imagine any of them 'taking advantage' of anybody?"

Marianne's imagination was better fueled than Adele's, and she started to walk faster, hurrying away from the mission ruins.

"Don't you want to have a party?" Adele persisted.

"I guess so, but why not a picnic, or something, with the family?"

"Oh, that's so boring, Marianne. No, I'm going to beg Mama for a Saturday night party, with ice cream, and dancing too."

Marianne shook her head. "Dad would never let me."

"Well, maybe just square dancing. That would be okay, wouldn't it?"

Marianne was unconvinced. She didn't want to spoil things for Adele, but she hoped that this time her father's old-fashioned ideas would prevail.

The next afternoon, the girls compared notes. "It's sure strange," Adele grumbled. "Our sixteenth birthdays, the most important birthday yet, and Mama says she 'doesn't have time' for a party."

"She's had a rough summer, with your papa gone, and then . . ." Marianne still found it hard to say his name. "Then her other troubles. But I thought surely my mother would agree, as long as we kept it simple. Of course, Dad did say 'no boys and no dancing.' But Mom just said maybe we'd have a family picnic after church on Sunday."

"Well, we'll just have to wheedle a little. I'll stop off this afternoon and help you persuade her."

But Carrie was adamant. "Anna isn't up to it, and I'm too busy. And I wouldn't even dare ask your father if you could have boys!"

Adele came over to sulk with Marianne on Saturday afternoon. "Happy birthday! Mama had the nerve to wish me a happy birthday this morning. What a laugh."

Though Marianne was secretly relieved that her mother hadn't approved Adele's idea, she was disappointed too. "You turn sixteen only once in your life, and nobody even seems to care."

Carrie seemed in a hurry to get the supper dishes done, but Marianne didn't think too much of it. When the phone rang, and her mother reported that Nancy wanted them to come over for the evening, she shrugged and muttered that she'd just as soon stay home.

"Now don't sulk, Marianne," her father chided. "Why don't you go upstairs and put on a pretty dress and come along?"

Marianne began to get suspicious when Ted and Liz both excused themselves on the grounds they had homework to do. When she saw Adele getting out of Anna's truck in Tim and Nancy's yard she was glad her mother had urged her to put on her new crepe shirtwaist with the jaunty bow at the neck.

"You two girls go on in," Matt urged. "We want to talk to Anna about something."

"Shoo." Anna waved toward the house. "We'll be along."

"Surprise! Surprise!" A chorus rang out as they entered the living room. Adele, who hadn't suspected a thing, gasped. Marianne grinned as she looked around the room. Not only their Fort Romie and Soledad friends, but most of the junior and senior classes from Gonzales High School were packed into the farmhouse.

Nancy and Tim stood in the kitchen doorway smiling as broadly as their guests.

The merry round of chatter and happy birthday greetings filled the old farmhouse for a while. As they subsided, Nancy came in from the kitchen and started them off on a round of charades. Adele quickly guessed Ernie's "Pack Up Your Troubles"; and Marianne laughed as heartily as anyone at George's impersonation of Charlie Chaplin in "Shoulder Arms."

One of the senior boys from Gonzales had spied the Victrola in the corner. He wound it up and put a record on, and toes started tapping to the "Merry Widow Waltz." Marianne saw the eagerness on Adele's face as some of the boys began moving furniture back against the wall. Surely her father wouldn't have approved of dancing, she thought. *I can't. He'd never let us have another party.*

She was right, much to Adele's chagrin. Tim came in from the kitchen with a scowl on his face, but Nancy took his arm. "Tim," she said softly. "Come help me serve the ice cream and cake."

"Thank God," Marianne whispered to Adele.

"For what?" Adele demanded. "It would have been fun."

"And Dad would have shut me up in the attic for the rest of my life."

"I guess so," Adele conceded. "And at least Nancy didn't let Tim embarrass us by causing a scene."

"What a letdown," Adele grumbled the following Saturday as she faced Marianne across the kitchen table.

"Last week, a great big party; this week, green tomato mincemeat."

"I kind of like making mincemeat," Marianne admitted, sniffing the pungent nutmeg she was grinding. "It always smells so good."

"Yes, but you've got the easy part. I have to chop all these tomatoes." She sighed and picked up the paring knife. "How did Lizzie get out of helping?"

"Mama let her go over to play with her girl friend. She said since we had a party last week, Liz was entitled to play today."

"The party was really great, wasn't it? I was so surprised."

"Me too. The way Dad always talks, I never dreamed he'd let us have a real boy-girl party."

"I think your mom had to talk him into it." Adele giggled. "But I'll bet it was Nancy's idea to begin with."

"It's nice to have someone around who's old enough for our folks to listen to, and young enough to understand, isn't it? Uncle Will and Aunt Irene aren't that much older, but they're so settled and stodgy."

"Yeah. Sometimes I forget Will's really my brother. He seems so old. But even you never call Tim 'uncle.' And can you imagine 'Aunt' Nancy?"

"Aunt Nancy! Since when am I old enough to be anybody's aunt, except, maybe, Sammy's?" Nancy smiled as she came into the kitchen, but Marianne noticed that she didn't seem as bouncy as usual. "Wow! Look at all those green tomatoes! I've got a bushel out in the car too. Do we have to peel them or just chop them up?"

"Just chop them, thank God. We have to peel the apples, though," Adele grumbled. "There's a couple of bushels in the root cellar. Mama and Carrie are out there getting them now."

Nancy found another paring knife in the big oak kitchen cabinet, sat down, and began dicing tomatoes into a dishpan.

"Not too small," Adele cautioned, "or they get mushy. Didn't you ever help your mother make preserves?"

"My mother always said it was easier to do it herself. She kept saying she'd teach me 'someday.'" She glanced out the window. Carrie and Anna were coming across the yard, carrying a bushel basket heaped with apples between them. "Do you girls know how lucky you are?" Nancy asked.

"I think I do," Adele said softly. "I know how much I miss Pa, and Eric too. I guess family's the most important thing we have."

Marianne felt her stomach knot at the mention of Eric's name.

"Speaking of Eric, has Anna ever heard anything from him?" Nancy asked sadly. "I still feel guilty about what happened. You know Tim and I never wanted to hurt him. If he hadn't been so sick, on top of the other. . ."

Marianne shivered. *I just can't stand it if they keep talking about him*, she thought. She stood, surprised that her shaking legs supported her. "I'll help Mom and Gran with the apples." She held the door wide as the older women stepped inside and dropped the heavy load. "I'll go get the rest of the apples," she told them as she let the door slam behind her.

She found the second basket of apples outside the sloping root cellar door and took a few moments to compose herself before she began dragging it toward the house. She was not really happy when Adele came out to help her.

Anna had one of the big blue enameled kettles on the stove and she stood stirring the tomatoes that were ready as Carrie and Nancy cored and peeled the green apples. Marianne and Adele sat and worked at the kitchen table. Soon a second kettle was filled, and Carrie took it to the stove.

The two girls chattered on about the latest fashions and about their surprise party, while their mothers stirred the mincemeat and they and Nancy listened. The delightful aroma of nutmeg, cinnamon, and cloves permeated the kitchen. Suddenly Nancy, who had been unusually quiet all morning, rose from the table with her hand over her mouth and quickly went into the bathroom.

Marianne started to get up. "I think she's sick. Maybe she needs help."

"Wait a few minutes," her mother advised. "I think she'll be all right soon."

Nancy did emerge very soon. "I'm sorry," she apologized. "It's just that I haven't been feeling real well the last few mornings anyhow, and the smell of all that food cooking just got to me."

Marianne wondered why her mother and Anna were smiling at each other. *If Nancy has whatever I had all summer, it's nothing to smile about,* she thought.

"Sick, mornings?" Carrie asked.

Nancy smiled, too, though a bit wanly. "Don't get too excited yet, you two. I'm a couple of weeks late, but I'm not sure yet."

"Does Tim know?" Anna asked.

"Know what?" Marianne whispered to Adele. "They act like being sick was a big joke."

"Silly," Adele whispered back. "Hasn't your mother told you anything? She's having a baby."

Chapter Eight

*C*arrie had taught Marianne how to make green tomato mincemeat, but she hadn't taught her that much about her own body. It was Adele, all excited about "being a woman" who had told her about starting her periods. When Marianne had had her first, her mother had seemed embarrassed. In most ways Carrie Hanlon was a modern woman, but she lacked the words to explain to her daughter the changes that were, although completely normal, so bewildering.

Marianne knew that, somehow, after a woman got married, something happened that caused a new life to grow within her. Married people did things you weren't supposed to know about until you were married yourself, and while she took part in the gossip of the other girls in school, they were nearly all as ignorant as she was.

But Marianne had grown up on a farm. She held scattered images in her memory—things nice girls didn't think about, much less talk about. Dogs coupled, and later there were puppies. Cows were bred and calved. Marianne was ignorant, but she was bright. The things she did know came together and produced a horrible truth.

There was no way she could hide her panic. She stumbled from the kitchen, blinded by tears and terror. Carrie and Anna were fussing over Nancy and didn't notice, but Adele raced upstairs after her.

She found her flung across her bed, sobbing hysterically. "Marianne, honey, what's the matter? Just because you didn't know . . . Lots of girls don't."

"Go away!"

"Not on your life," Adele vowed. "Something has you terribly upset, and it isn't that Nancy and Tim are going to have a baby."

"Please, Adele," Marianne pleaded through her sobs. "Please go away and leave me alone."

"Not until you tell me what's wrong and let me help you."

"There's nothing you can do to help me." Marianne shouted, but the words were muffled by her pillow. "There isn't anything anybody can do to help me," she wailed.

Adele sat on the bed, smoothing Marianne's auburn curls. "Nothing's that bad, Marianne. If you won't tell me, I'll get your mother."

"No!" Sobs wracked her again, and through them she begged, "Whatever you do, don't you dare call my mother. Promise me," she demanded.

"Then tell me what's wrong."

Marianne turned her swollen face from the pillow. "You have to promise never to tell anyone—not my mother or your mother or anyone—not a living soul."

Adele hesitated. Marianne's tortured eyes looked at her. "All right," she agreed at last. "I won't tell."

Marianne turned her face to the wall. Adele had to strain to hear the whispered words. "I, I think I'm going to have a baby too."

Quiet tears poured from her now. It was almost a relief. Adele tried to protest. "Lots of girls miss periods sometimes," she soothed. "Lots of girls get upset stomachs."

Marianne's sobs didn't ease.

"But how?" Adele persisted. "You never let any of the boys get the least bit fresh."

Marianne would not tell Adele everything. She couldn't tell Adele that her own half brother could be so evil. She could only cry and cry and cry, and Adele began to cry with her.

That was how Carrie found them, lying arm in arm on Marianne's bed, weeping. "Marianne, Adele, what in the world is the matter with you two? We were all downstairs in the kitchen congratulating Nancy, and suddenly the two of you have run off and are up here crying your eyes out. Come on, it's good news."

Adele let go of Marianne and sat up. "It's Marianne. She, she doesn't feel well, and I came up to see if I could help."

"Marianne." Her mother shook her gently. "Marianne, does it hurt? Should I call the doctor?"

Her daughter shook her head emphatically.

"But if you're sick, he can help," Carrie coaxed. "Did she tell you what was wrong, Adele?"

The girl bit her lip and nodded.

"Then tell me. Come on, Adele, tell me what's wrong."

"I can't. I promised."

"Promised? But I'm her mother. I can't help her if I don't know what's wrong. Marianne." She caressed the girl's shoulder. "Marianne, look at me."

But Marianne burrowed deeper into her tear-stained pillow. Carrie turned again to Adele, who looked from mother to daughter. "Marianne, I can't tell her, because I promised not to. But you have to. She's going to find out anyhow, eventually, and she's the only one who can help."

The curls on the back of Marianne's head shook. "No one can help. My life is ruined, forever, and nobody can help," she sobbed into the pillow.

"Adele," Carrie motioned toward the door, "maybe if you left us alone for a while? Since you can't break your word."

Adele left, and Carrie sat on the edge of the bed. "Marianne, whatever is bothering you seems like the end of the world, I know. But it isn't. You're just sixteen, and your whole life is in front of you. Tell Mother what's hurting you so."

I can't tell her, Marianne thought. *I can't ruin their lives too. Maybe I'll wait until tonight, when they've gone to bed, and then run away.*

"Honey, are you sick? Does your stomach hurt, or your head?"

The curls shook again.

"Then is it someone else? Did you hear that one of your friends is sick?"

"No!"

"Someone hurt your feelings? Is there some gossip that Adele told you?"

Marianne turned toward her mother. "No, I'm not sick, and none of my friends is sick. And my feelings aren't hurt."

"Then tell me why you're lying up here crying your eyes out," Carrie demanded.

Marianne heard the impatience creeping into her mother's voice. "Marianne," Carrie continued, "nothing is bad enough for all this fuss. Now, out with it."

Marianne had always been an obedient child, and she really couldn't run away. Adele was right. Her mother was going to find out eventually. "Nancy isn't the only one who's going to have a baby," she choked.

Carrie frowned, puzzled rather than angry, her daughter realized. "Marianne, whatever are you talking about?"

"I was sick all summer, Mama, but I didn't know what it was, and I didn't want you to worry."

Carrie smiled gently. "Being sick to your stomach doesn't necessarily mean you're having a baby. I guess I should have talked to you more about things like that. I'm sorry I didn't. It was hard for me. But, Marianne, if you've been sick, you should have told me. We'd have gone to the doctor, and he would have given you something to make you feel better."

"I haven't had my period for two months," the girl blurted.

Carrie nodded. "I had noticed, but that's not un-usual for young girls. I stopped and started a few times when I was your age too." She wiped Marianne's wet face with her apron. "But, Marianne, you can't be having a baby. You have to be with a man." She fumbled awkwardly, searching for the words. "It's like . . . Remember, in the Bible, how the angel came to Mary, and she asked how she could have a baby, because she wasn't married yet?"

"But she did have a baby."

"That was Mary, and that was Jesus. You know the difference. It just doesn't happen that way."

Marianne nodded. "I know." She wept again, remembering the June twilight and the mission ruins. When she looked at her mother again, she knew Carrie believed her. But she didn't hate her. She reached out a mother's arms and cradled Marianne in them, mingling her own tears with her daughter's.

They weren't aware that the other women had finished the mincemeat and gone home after Adele had assured them that Marianne was "just a little under the weather." Liz found them, still sitting on the bed, when she got home in mid-afternoon. Carrie jumped when her younger daughter came into the room.

"Gee, Mom, what's the matter?"

"Your sister's feeling sick," Carrie explained. "There are some pork chops in the ice box. Why don't you go down and start supper?"

She turned back to Marianne. "You don't want to go downstairs, do you?" she soothed. "I'll bring up some supper for you later, and some warm water so you can clean up."

"We have to tell Daddy, don't we?"

Carrie nodded slowly. "I'm afraid so. It won't be easy, but remember, no matter what he says, he loves you. We both do. You know that, don't you?"

Marianne sniffed and dabbed at her puffy eyes. "How can you, when I've disgraced you so?"

Carrie's arms tightened around the girl again. "Marianne, what has happened is disgraceful, and, if you really are carrying a child, these next months will be the hardest you, or any of us, will ever have to live through. But I can't believe you've done anything to disgrace us, or yourself. When you're ready, you will tell me exactly what happened, and who did this to you. But for now, I trust you, and I know you were innocent."

Carrie knocked softly, and then entered the bedroom carrying a tray with a basin of warm water and a bowl of steaming soup.

"Did you tell Daddy?" Marianne asked.

"Not yet. Marianne, I've been thinking, and what I said before is still true. The stomach trouble could have been nerves, and young girls do miss their periods for no reason. I think you should see a doctor before we get your father all upset."

"Oh, Mama, if only it weren't true. Mom, I'd give anything if I were wrong."

"I hope and pray you are."

"But you don't really think so, do you?"

Carrie didn't answer. She took the soft cloth in her hand and began bathing her daughter's face. "We'll pray to God and we'll go see Dr. Smith on Monday."

"Dr. Smith? Do we have to? Couldn't we go to someone we don't know?"

Carrie thought for a few minutes and then nodded.
"We'll go down to King City. Nobody down there knows
us."

The doctor in King City was a stranger. Though his
words were kind, his eyes were still judgmental. Young
girls whose mothers brought them to him from twenty
miles away were usually girls "in trouble."

"I'm sorry," he told them when he had finished the
examination, which had frightened Marianne almost as
much as Eric's assault. "At least she is a healthy girl and
everything seems quite normal." He spoke to Carrie as if
Marianne weren't there. "I would guess the baby is due
about the end of March."

Deep down inside, Marianne actually felt a little
relief. Mama shared her secret now, and Mama was taking
charge. Surely her mother would find some answer. *But
that's stupid*, she admitted to herself. *Babies don't go away,
and a girl who has a baby and no husband is forever disgraced.*

The nurse said something to Carrie, but she spoke so
softly Marianne hadn't heard the first few words. "She's
careful, and she's completely trustworthy," the nurse told
her. "But it would have to be done quite soon."

Carrie shook her head firmly. "No, I knew a girl once
who did that. It killed her."

"This woman is very good."

Carrie shook her head again firmly. "It's very dangerous, and besides, something in me just says that it's
wrong—very, very wrong."

The nurse shrugged. "Well, if you change your mind, give me a call."

"Marianne," her mother said as she drove out of King City, "are you ready to tell me who it was?"

Marianne bit her lip and tried once more to hold back her tears. "Does it really matter?" she choked. "It won't change anything."

"It might," her mother said gently. "If it is one of the boys in town, the best thing might be for you to marry him. I know you're young, but it would protect you, both of you. If he's a decent boy at all, he'd want to take care of you. Was it George Pelham? Was that why you didn't want to be near him last summer?"

"Oh, no, Mom. It wasn't George."

"Ernie? Bill?"

"It wasn't any of the boys from school, Mom."

Carrie was counting backward, as every woman learns to do. "June," she said.

June, Marianne thought. *Just last June. It was such a happy day. My first grown-up dress, my hair curled, being a bridesmaid.* She shuddered.

"Marianne, I can understand how hard it must be to talk about it." She was silent for a few miles. "Marianne, I do understand. A man hurt me very much once, too, not the same way this man hurt you, thank God, but he did use me. So I do know something about how you feel. But believe me, protecting him is not what you should do. He doesn't deserve it. He is responsible for what has happened to you, and he should be held accountable."

"He, he doesn't live around here," she stammered.

"Was it a stranger, then?" Carrie probed. "Someone you didn't know? You should have come to us right away. Men who do things like that to girls can be sent to prison, Marianne."

"Mom, he was sick. I don't think he meant to hurt me. He didn't know what he was doing."

"I doubt that," Carrie answered sharply. "Marianne, this man doesn't deserve your protection. Please tell me who it was."

"He's gone away, Mom. It would only hurt more people . . ."

"Then it was someone you knew."

Marianne saw her mother's eyes go wide and her mouth open in shock. "Oh, no! Marianne, tell me what I am thinking isn't true."

Marianne couldn't say the words, couldn't bring herself to say the name. As they turned into the farmyard, her mother spoke with the saddest voice Marianne had ever heard. "It was Eric, wasn't it?"

Marianne's silence confirmed her mother's fears. "Oh, dear God, help us. How can we ever tell Anna?"

Chapter Nine

*M*att must have been watching for the car, because Carrie and Marianne had scarcely come through the front door when they heard the back one slam behind him. He was still drying his rough, strong hands when he met them in the living room. "Well, you were gone a long time. What did the doctor say?" He looked at their solemn faces. "It isn't anything serious, is it?"

Marianne edged toward the stairs, but her mother stopped her. "I'm sorry, Marianne, but it won't be any easier later." The girl sagged into Carrie's sewing rocker.

"You'd better sit down, Matt," Carrie sighed. "I'm afraid we have a lot of talking to do."

Matt twisted the coarse bleached sacking towel. He stood beside the rocker, put a hand on his daughter's shoulder, and looked at his wife impatiently. "But she's never been sick. What did Dr. Smith say, Carrie?"

"We, ah, we didn't go to Dr. Smith," Carrie said. "We went down to King City."

"But why? Dr. Smith's been our doctor ever since he came to town. Carrie, don't keep me standing here worrying. What's wrong with my little girl?"

Tears were spilling from Marianne's eyes again. She sniffed, and her father handed the towel to her. "There, there, honey. Dry your eyes. It can't be as bad as all that. We'll do whatever it takes. You'll be fine." He sat down on the edge of the chintz-covered sofa. "Carrie, tell me."

"Please, Matt." Carrie paced the room trying to find the words. "Matt, it wasn't Marianne's fault. Please remember that, and don't be angry with her."

"Angry!" he roared. "Why should I be angry? Of course, it isn't her fault if she's sick. Now, Carrie, tell me what's going on here. Tell me right now."

"Marianne's not sick, exactly. The doctor says she's very healthy, in fact, but . . ."

"Then why are you sitting there scaring me half to death, for Pete's sake?" He looked from wife to daughter.

Marianne finally broke the silence. "I'm going to have a baby."

"What?" Matt exploded. Then, after what seemed like an eternity of listening to Marianne's soft sobs and Carrie's footsteps as she walked back and forth between them, he continued with surprising gentleness. "Marianne, that's impossible. I must not have heard right." He looked at Carrie, who only nodded.

"But how?" Matt muttered. "Who?"

Neither mother nor daughter spoke.

"Tell me who." Matt kept his voice low, but its intensity echoed in the little room. "Tell me who did this to you. I swear he'll do his duty by you, or I'll kill him with my own two hands."

When he received no answer he probed. "George? If that Pelham kid dared to take liberties with you . . ."

"Please, Daddy, it wasn't George," Marianne pleaded. "It wasn't any of the boys around here."

"Some no good tramp!" Matt's voice rose. "Some bum. At the rodeo?" he asked. "Where was Tim? He was supposed to be looking after you!"

"It didn't happen at the rodeo, Matt," Carrie sighed. "It was before that. It was in June, right after the wedding."

"The wedding?" He thought for a moment. "After Tim and Nancy's wedding?" he asked.

Marianne nodded.

"Did you know the man, Marianne?"

Why does he want me to say the words my soul hates so? Can't he figure it out? She nodded again.

"Matt," Carrie interrupted, "she didn't understand. He forced her."

Matt's face was livid, but he struggled to keep his voice gentle. "Marianne, I love you, and I can't believe you're a bad girl, but what were you doing alone with a man? You must have known it was dangerous."

"Matt, she had no reason to distrust him."

"Then you know who it was, Carrie? How long have you known about this—this monster?"

"I only found out yesterday, Matt, and I only learned who it was this afternoon."

"Marianne, if you were . . . " the words he knew, he was ashamed to use in front of his wife and daughter, "hurt," he hedged, "why didn't you tell us right away?"

Marianne stared into her lap, and her mother spoke. "Matt, she was afraid, and ashamed."

"I didn't want anyone to know, Daddy. It was terrible, and I just wanted to forget it all."

"Marianne, he should be locked up and never let out for doing such a thing to an innocent girl. You've got to tell me who it was."

"What good would that do, Daddy?"

"Are you trying to protect him, honey? He doesn't deserve it. He can be made to do right by you."

"He's gone away, Daddy, and . . ." She thought of Anna, who treated her like a daughter. "It would hurt someone else. Besides, he was sick, and hurt, and he didn't know what he was doing. And he's gone away, and I pray to God he never comes back."

"I don't care if he was sick, and right now I'd just as soon he was dead, but Marianne, for your sake, you've got to tell me who hurt you. If you protect him it makes you look guilty."

"Matt," Carrie inserted gently, "she isn't protecting the man. It's his family."

"A married man!" Matt's fists clenched. "Then his wife should know what a good-for-nothing bum she has for a husband."

"Matt, please." Carrie sat down next to her husband and took his arm. "Matt, it would hurt our own family. It would tear us apart."

Watching his face, Marianne couldn't imagine the horrible thoughts that passed through her father's mind before he came to the name he spoke through taut lips. "Eric? Oh, no!" He buried his face in his hands.

"You see, Matt," Carrie said. "We can't tell Anna. She's so upset as it is by his leaving, and this would break her heart."

It was Matt who first slipped to his knees. When his wife and daughter knelt beside him, he put a sinewy arm around each and poured out his heart to the only friend he could ask for help.

"Ted and Lizzie will be home from school soon," Carrie reminded them, as she rose stiffly. "I don't think we should say anything to them for now at least."

Matt nodded, and Marianne dried her eyes on the hand towel she still held. "Mama," she said softly, "may I please go upstairs?"

"Of course you may," Carrie replied. "I'll bring you some supper if you'd rather not come downstairs later."

Marianne shook her head. "I'm really not hungry, Mama. But could you keep Lizzie down here, please? I just want to be alone for a little while."

"I'll handle your sister, Marianne, but I will bring you some supper," Carrie promised. "And we'll figure out something."

"Yes, honey, we'll find some way to protect you." Her father hugged her, and she almost believed him.

"I told Liz you were sick and not to bother you," Carrie explained when she brought up the supper tray. "But, Marianne, we can't keep putting everyone off. Your sister and brother are worried about you, and so, I'm sure, are Anna and the rest of the family."

"We can't tell them, Mom," Marianne insisted. "We can't tell anyone, especially not Gran."

"Your father thinks we should tell Anna and try to find Eric, Marianne."

"Oh, no! Never."

"It isn't as if he were really your uncle, honey. You could be married."

"No, Mama."

"It would save you from being shamed and give your child a name, and a father."

"No, Mom." Her voice was firm. "I don't know what to do, but I will not do that. Any life at all would be better than that. Please don't ever make me even see him again."

Carrie smoothed the curls back from her daughter's forehead. "Eat some supper, and then try to get a little rest. I'll talk to your father tonight, and tomorrow we'll all decide what to do."

Marianne stayed in bed until Liz and Ted had left for school the next morning. Then she dressed and dragged herself downstairs. Her parents sat at the kitchen table. One glance told her that neither had slept the night before. As she slipped into one of the high-backed oak chairs, Carrie offered her a bowl of oatmeal and milk, but the girl ignored the food.

"Mama, I've been thinking all night—ever since Saturday, really, but there is so much I don't know. The nurse, yesterday at the doctor's office, what was she talking about?"

"Nothing, Marianne. Nothing you need to know about."

"But it's my life, Mama. I wish I could just let you and Daddy take care of me, always, but I can't."

"She's right," Matt agreed. "She has a right to know her options."

"That isn't an option," Carrie insisted. "I will not see my daughter hurt more than she's already been hurt."

"Mom, you're always saying we have to learn to make our own decisions," Marianne reminded her. "This is the most important decision I'll ever make. You two can't make it for me, much as I wish you could." She looked from one despairing face to the other. "But I have to have your help."

"Just what did the nurse suggest?" Matt asked. "Does she know someone?"

"Yes," Carrie answered reluctantly. "She says there is a woman there, in King City."

"I've heard talk." Matt fiddled with a corner of the table cloth. "Men talk about these things, too, you know. They say there are ways."

Marianne looked at them in bewilderment. They were talking as if she weren't even there. She remembered how when she was a little girl, they used to spell things out so she wouldn't understand. "Please, Mom, Dad, you're talking in riddles. Ways to do what?"

"Ways to . . . There are ways to . . ." Matt looked helplessly at Carrie.

"Ways to get rid of the baby, Marianne." Carrie went on hastily. "But it's a terrible thing to do. I knew a girl once in San Francisco. She got in trouble, and she went to a doctor. Not just some woman in a back alley, but a doctor. But she got the fever, and she died."

Marianne wondered if death were the worst thing that could happen, but her mother was still speaking. "It was a terrible way to die. She lingered for days, in agony. She was sure God was punishing her."

"Hush," Matt protested. "It's done all the time, and most do fine."

"Yes," Carrie admitted. "It's done all the time, but she suffered so."

"The doctor said he could hear the baby's heart, Mom. He said in a few weeks I'll be able to hear it too," Marianne said thoughtfully. "I wouldn't care if I did die, really I wouldn't. What do I have to live for anyhow? But . . ."

"You have your whole life ahead of you," Matt interrupted. "You have school to finish and nursing school if you really want to go. You have marriage, a good, loving marriage, and a real family of your own to look forward to."

Marianne shook her head sadly. "Daddy, I can't go on with school. I couldn't face people. And I won't be able to get into any good nursing school. And no decent boy will want to marry me."

Matt opened his mouth in protest, but the girl went on. "No, I don't care what happens to me, but the baby didn't do anything wrong. It didn't ask to happen, but it's already a baby, isn't it? How can it be right to kill it before it even has a chance to be born?"

"Honey, you have to think of yourself," Matt said gently. "It isn't really a baby yet. There's no life in it yet."

"Matthew," Carrie protested, "you have not carried a baby within you. I have. Maybe I loved them more because they were your children, but I loved them, each one, long before I felt life in them." She looked at her daughter proudly. "My friend died in agony because she believed God was punishing her for killing her baby. I don't know about that. I do believe God is forgiving. But I also think what she did was wrong."

"Daddy, I'll do it if you want me to, but . . ."

"No, Marianne." He pushed the chair back and stood. "No, you'll not risk your life and your conscience to take what looks like an easy way out. We'll find a better answer. God help us, if it means selling out and leaving the valley, we'll find a better way."

Somehow, life went on. Marianne could not bring herself to face school, and her parents didn't pressure her. The neighbors accepted the simple statement that Marianne wasn't well. After all, tuberculosis and rheumatic fever afflicted thousands, and many households sheltered an invalid.

Adele knew about the baby, but, though she was a born gossip, her love for Marianne kept her quiet. If she made wild guesses about the baby's father, she kept them to herself. Only once, on one of her frequent visits, did she dare question her best friend.

"Linda quit school to get married," she reported. "Of course everybody thinks she's having a baby." Adele inspected her hands. "Marianne, why don't you get married? People would talk for a while, but then they'd forget. But if you don't get married, then they'll call you awful names, and . . ."

"I can't get married," Marianne told her. "And I wouldn't, even if I could."

"You hate him, don't you?"

"I've tried not to, Adele. I've tried to forgive him, but I can't. And I don't want to talk about him, ever."

Adele never brought up the subject again.

The holidays were approaching, and still no decision had been made. "The family will think it's funny if you aren't at Thanksgiving dinner," Carrie mused one morning when they were alone in the house.

Marianne glanced at her thickening waist. "I can't, Mama. They'll know." She looked out the window at the steady drip of the November rain and thought how she'd like to go outside again and walk in the fresh air, in spite of the cold. "Mama, it's time."

"Maybe if we made you some new clothes . . ."

"Mom, everybody thinks I have some awful disease. I should be wasting away." She smiled ruefully. "Instead, I'm getting fatter and fatter. No, Mom. It's time for me to go away."

It wasn't as if they hadn't talked about it. First they'd talked about selling the farm and moving, but Marianne wouldn't hear of that. "I can't make a mess of everyone's life," she'd protested. "Take Ted and Lizzie away from their friends; make you give up your good farm; walk out on Anna and Will and Tim."

She looked out the window again and across the valley that had always been her home. "You know it's the only thing to do, Mom. And Dad knows too."

"But where? If only we had someone who could look after you. I do have one old friend in San Francisco." Carrie smiled as she remembered dear Betsy. "She has a family of her own now, and her mother-in-law lives with them too. But I could write."

"Mom, remember when the Salvation Army people were here last spring, raising money for the needy?"

"And you announced that you were going to become a nurse and go off with the Salvation Army and be a missionary?" Carrie smiled indulgently. "Maybe someday, though I must admit I hope not. But now?"

"Don't they have places where girls can go? They'd be kind to me, and they'd take care of my baby."

"The Army." Carrie smiled again. "They always seem to have an answer, don't they?"

"Maybe I could come home afterward," Marianne said wistfully. "Maybe I could come home, and things could be like they used to be, or almost."

Matt had seemed, for months, to be bearing the weight of the world on his broad shoulders. When Carrie and Marianne told him of their plan, he looked as if the weight had been taken away. He smiled, as Carrie had, and repeated her words almost exactly. "The Salvation Army. Praise the Lord for them. They always seem to have an answer."

Marianne had tuberculosis, they told the family. As she'd been sick since summer, no one doubted the lie. Now the doctor thought she'd get better if she went to a drier climate, at least for the winter. "Before Christmas?" Anna had protested. But of course if it would help her get well, the sooner she left the better.

They so bundled her up when they left for the railroad station, as an invalid should be, that no one could have guessed their secret. And her rosy cheeks were seen as another symptom, from the fever. She cried, and the family thought it was because she was saying good-bye.

"I love you all so," she told them and meant it. "I'll miss you terribly."

On the train Marianne wriggled out of the heavy overcoat and settled into the worn seat. Carrie sat next to her and took her hand. "That was the hardest part," she assured her daughter. "At least now you won't have to pretend."

"I hated lying to them, Mama. I know it's wrong to lie, but the truth would hurt them so."

"I hate lying to them, too, but I can't believe it's wrong. The Bible says 'thou shalt not bear false witness against thy neighbor.' But who are we bearing false witness against?"

"I tried that once on you, when I was a little girl, and you didn't buy it."

Carrie squeezed Marianne's cold hand. "I probably didn't, but when the truth can only hurt, and the lie can protect everyone—you, your baby, Anna—how can the lie be wrong? And if it is, God knows our hearts. God knows. If this lie is a sin, he will forgive us all."

The train chugged through Salinas, over the rocky hills, and into the Santa Clara Valley. San Jose was bigger than any city Marianne had ever seen. She strained to spot the normal school where Nancy had gone to become a teacher.

In San Jose, they changed trains and rode on through the fields that fringed San Francisco Bay. Oakland—Oakland was, for now, a refuge. *But then what?* Marianne wondered. *After we get to Oakland, and Mom goes back home to Soledad, and I'm all alone, then what?*

Chapter Ten

To a girl from the country, the big, old building on the busy street wasn't reassuring, but the smile of the gray-haired woman who opened the door put Marianne's fears at ease. "Oh, my, yes. We were expecting you, Marianne. And Mrs. Hanlon . . ." She took Carrie's right hand in hers as she patted Marianne's shoulder with her left.

As the woman, who'd introduced herself simply as Mattie, led them across a sparsely furnished parlor, Marianne heard voices and saw several young women sewing in an adjoining room. Across the hall, a few younger girls seemed to be studying.

Mattie must have noticed her glance. "A teacher comes from the high school, so our girls can keep up with their lessons if they wish."

"I've been studying some at home," Marianne told her. "But I hadn't dared hope I could keep up with my class. I . . . I would so love to graduate with my friends next year."

Major Hudson rose from her desk and stretched out her arms in welcome as they entered the cramped office. "Please excuse the mess," she apologized. "We're building a new hospital, as you've probably heard, and I'm swamped with record keeping and fund raising. But our girls still come first." The way she smiled convinced Marianne she meant what she said. "First, let me ask you a few questions—for our medical records mostly. Then I'll show you around."

The doctor from King City had sent his report as they had requested, and Major Hudson glanced at it briefly. "I'm happy to see that there don't appear to be any medical difficulties. Our facilities are good, but somewhat limited, and if there are complications we sometimes have to call in outside doctors or send the girls to a larger hospital for their confinement."

She paused and studied Marianne and her mother. "Forgive me if my questions seem too personal, but it helps, sometimes, if I know a girl's circumstances." She leaned across the desk and took Marianne's hands. "May I ask why you've come to us? You aren't alone, obviously, and you don't appear destitute. In fact, your mother's letter offers to pay your expenses. I don't ask this to pry, but in your circumstances most girls marry the child's father. I gather that isn't possible for you?"

Marianne shook her head firmly as Carrie explained. "The man has disappeared. He, he was connected to our family, closely, and he . . ." She tried to go on, but Major Hudson interrupted gently.

"I think I understand all I need to know. I'm sure Mattie has sent your trunk up to your room by now,

Marianne, so why don't we get you settled. You must be tired from your train trip. Since most of the girls are in classes right now, you might like to take a little nap before meeting everyone."

Marianne was thankful that Major Hudson had invited her mother to stay for supper that first night. Young women—most in their teens and nearly all obviously pregnant—filled the long tables in the dining hall. Marianne, who had somehow thought no one else felt her shame and fear, wondered if she could ever share their easy friendship.

She smiled as she studied Major Hudson. Marianne and her mother had been seated at the table she headed. At the other tables, Marianne noticed, everyone seemed to talk at once, chattering and giggling. But the major controlled the conversation at her table, encouraging each girl to introduce herself to the newcomer.

She'd met Edith briefly and knew they would share a room. Edith's pinched face showed hunger and so did her darting black eyes, which avoided everyone else's. Only the major seemed to be able to force the girl to meet her patient, motherly look.

She said, in response to the major's prodding, only that her name was Edith and that she had lived all her life in Oakland. She'd come to Beulah Home only a few weeks before; her baby was due right after New Year's. When the major asked her what she hoped to do after that, she shrugged thin shoulders. "I hope I can get a job somewhere, maybe in a store. It would be nice to work around pretty things, even if you couldn't afford to own them."

Sarah was about Marianne's age. She volunteered that her boyfriend was coming back to get her as soon as he "found a good job," and Marianne didn't miss the knowing glances of their tablemates. Major Hudson nodded. "I do hope so, Sarah, and pray so."

Jade seemed a strange name for a strange girl. Marianne had never seen a Chinese girl before. She had seen a few men working in the fields or on the railroad but no women. Jade was rather pretty. Her dark eyes didn't actually slant, like people said, though they were an interesting almond shape, wide set and deep. She had high cheekbones and a small nose. And her coal-black, short, straight hair set off her creamy skin.

"Jade is shy with strangers," Major Hudson explained. "She's afraid her English isn't good enough, but she studies hard."

Jade was not pregnant. *Perhaps she's already had her baby,* Marianne thought. *Maybe I can get to know her and get her to tell me about China.*

Neither Edith nor Sarah attended the high school classes. Edith already had her diploma, and Sarah saw no future in schooling. "I'm going to get married real soon," she insisted. Most of the girls giggled and turned away. Marianne understood that many of them had been told the same stories by the fathers of their own babies. And they had believed them, for a while. She prayed that Sarah's faith was better placed, and thanked God that at least she hadn't been deluded.

Every day Jade sat in the little classroom with Marianne. The teacher provided her with first and second grade McGuffey readers, and her almond eyes pored over the vaguely familiar letters. Though she apologized often for her English, she spoke it well enough that she and Marianne soon became friends.

Jade tried to keep up with the lessons the other girls were being taught, too, but her limited English made it hard for her to follow things like geometry and chemistry. Marianne enjoyed spending her free time helping Jade with her English, and Jade shyly confided in her.

"I went, for a little while, to the missionary's school," she explained. "Just a little while; I learned not much—a few simple words of English, a little bit about Jesus. Then the soldiers came and took the crops. My mother died. My father had to sell me, to get food for my brothers."

"Sell you!"

"It is done there," Jade said flatly. "It must be done. Otherwise, everyone starves. If I had not been sold, I would have starved."

"But how did you get here?" Marianne asked. "If you were born in China, how did you get to America?"

Jade shook her head. "That is too long a story, and, yes, too unhappy. It is enough that I am here now, and the good people of the Salvation Army help me to study so that I can learn more about Jesus and then teach to others what I have learned."

Christmas Day was not a merry day at Beulah Home. Major Hudson and the other Salvation Army people did their best. They put up a big tree in the parlor, and the girls popped corn and made paper chains to trim it. There were one or two presents for each of the young women, gifts from strangers, but welcome things, like hairbrushes and sweaters.

Marianne and a few others received boxes from home and shared homemade ginger cookies, fruitcake, and fudge. Carrie had put some extra packages in with the clothes she had sent her daughter, and Marianne happily handed out books for Jade, a soft silk blouse for Edith, and a fluffy quilt for Sarah, who was still determined to keep her baby.

It was Jade's first American Christmas, and she seemed overwhelmed by the celebration. "But if it is Jesus' birthday," she asked, "why are there no gifts offered him? In China, on the days we honor the gods, we clothe the idols and leave food for the spirits. But for Jesus' day, gifts are given, instead, to us."

"But he doesn't need anything," Marianne told her new friend. "Since he commanded us to love one another, this is how we honor him, by showing our love to the ones he loves."

"Well put, Marianne," Major Hudson said.

"I do wish I could have honored Jesus this way," Jade said with a sigh. "But I have nothing to give."

"But you do," Marianne protested. "You're always giving, every day. You're always taking someone's place in the kitchen, or helping someone who's feeling ill with her cleaning."

"But that is only my duty," Jade insisted. "This has become my home and these girls my family. I only hope that when I have studied enough, I can repay to the Salvation Army what they have given me."

"What do you plan to do when you leave here?" Marianne asked Jade later that afternoon, when most of the girls had scattered to their own rooms. "You're not having a baby, like most of us. Did you have one? Is that why you came here?"

Jade stared at her hands, avoiding Marianne's eyes. "I ran away. The man who owned me brought me here, to America, and I ran away. I had no place else to go. I heard the band, on the street, and I remembered the song, from before, from China. So I went to them, and they brought me here."

"But you can't stay here forever."

"How I wish I could, Marianne. But, of course, that isn't possible. That is why I must study hard. Then I will become one of them, a soldier in Jesus' Army, and I will help others."

"I think . . ." Marianne spoke slowly and thoughtfully. "I think I will join the Salvation Army, too, after my baby is born. I've always wanted to be a nurse," she mused. "I can join the Salvation Army and become an officer and still be a nurse. That way I can help other girls."

The loud clang of the doorbell cut into their talk. Jade jumped up and opened the door a crack. Marianne could see the man—boy, really—who stood on the porch. "I'm looking for Sarah," she heard him say. "Her ma told me they sent her here. Could you please tell her Jimmy's come?"

Few stories at Beulah Home had as happy an ending as Sarah's. Edith had her baby just a week later, on New Year's Day, and signed the papers giving it up for adoption. "What else could I do?" she asked, shrugging, the day she returned to the room she shared with Marianne.

Marianne felt her own child kick, sharply. She sighed. "It's best. Everyone says so, Edith. It's what I must do, too, I guess." The baby inside her stretched. "Was it a boy or a girl?" she asked.

"I don't know." Edith, who'd seemed so cold and bitter before, brushed a tear from her eye. "Oh, Marianne, I couldn't bear to ask."

"I know." Marianne looked at her swelling body. "They say we mustn't see them, mustn't let ourselves get too attached." She forced a strangled laugh. "Not get attached. Isn't that absurd?"

Edith left a few weeks later. The Salvation Army had found a job for her doing alterations in one of the fine department stores downtown. "So my time wasn't totally wasted here," she had muttered while packing. "At least I learned to sew well enough to earn a living."

Marianne had a new roommate, an older girl named Ardis, whose baby was due about the same time as Marianne's. When she was with the others, Ardis kept up a good front. She was attentive in sewing classes; she bowed her head reverently when Major Hudson asked the blessing before meals; she even went to Corps Meeting on Sundays.

But she dropped the facade when she and Marianne were alone in their room. "Isn't it mean?" she grumbled. "You know those old hens just whisper about us behind our backs. 'Those poor, poor, wayward girls.' Ha! Who do they think they're kidding? They know it's their own husbands that use us, take what they can get, and then when they get us in trouble, off they go."

Marianne's mouth dropped open in shock. "But they're only helping us—giving us a place to go, protecting us."

"Your first time, I gather."

"Whatever do you mean? How would any girl let such a thing happen twice?"

"Accidents happen. Maybe you don't mean it to happen. A guy takes you out for dinner; he expects his due; he's got 'protection' but it don't always work. So there you are, out on the street."

"Accident?" Marianne couldn't understand Ardis's attitude. What had happened to her was no accident. "But Ardis," she protested, "a baby is no accident. It takes a deliberate act. Aren't you at all sorry that you're having a baby without being married?"

"I suppose you are? Come on, if you're so innocent, how come you're in the same fix I am?"

Marianne had often wondered that and prayed for God's forgiveness for her unknown sin. But now, accused, she became defensive. "He forced me," she told an incredulous Ardis.

"Sure, sure. Okay, if that's the way you want it, sweetie. Maybe, one time in a hundred or so."

"You've been awfully quiet today," Major Hudson said to Marianne after supper that evening. "Is something bothering you? If you'd like to talk about it . . ."

Marianne hesitated, but the older woman's smile was so kind. "Come into the office. We can be alone there."

She closed the door behind them. "Now, sit down and tell me all about it."

"Major Hudson, I didn't mean for this to happen, but it did, and I must have done something wrong. Do you think God will ever forgive me?"

"Have you asked him to?" the older woman inquired gently.

"Oh, yes, over and over." She thought of Ardis's heartless words. "But, Major Hudson, I don't think I've really repented. I mean . . ."

Major Hudson didn't even look shocked. She just waited for Marianne to go on.

"Major Hudson, I want to, really I do. But how can I repent when I can't understand what I did wrong? I know I must have done something to encourage him. I must have. Oh, I know it must never happen again, but I've gone over and over the whole awful thing in my mind, and I still don't know what I did wrong."

"Marianne, have you ever told anyone exactly what happened to you?" When Marianne slowly shook her head, she added, "Then would you like to tell me?" She put a strong arm around Marianne and drew her close.

Marianne sobbed as she poured out the story of that hour at the old mission. "He was sick, and I guess he was drunk," Marianne concluded. "But I must have done something to encourage him."

"You poor child," the older woman murmured as she smoothed Marianne's hair. "I really don't think there's anything for God to forgive you for. Marianne, what happened to you is a crime, a vicious crime called rape. The one who needs forgiveness is the man who did this to you, and I marvel at the strength God has given you to forgive him. At the very worst you are guilty of trusting too much and, maybe, a little poor judgment for following him alone. Now what you must do, I think, is to forgive yourself."

Marianne let the motherly woman comfort her for a few moments. "Thank you," she said at last. "Thank you for not blaming me." But she hadn't forgotten Ardis's words. There would be those who would understand, like Major Hudson, and her mother. But there would be the others too. Maybe one day she would forgive herself, but there would always be someone out there who would look down on her.

Chapter Eleven

*M*ama!" Marianne tried to stifle the cry, but the pain was too great.

"It's all right," Carrie crooned. "Mama's here, and everything will be all right. I know it hurts, but it will be over soon."

Marianne gasped and turned her face toward the bare wall as another spasm of pain gripped her. When it passed she turned back toward her mother. "I'm so scared, Mama. They told me it would hurt, but . . ." Another contraction came, bringing another cry.

Carrie pressed a damp cloth to her daughter's forehead. Marianne realized her mother was crying, and fought to hold back her own screams. "I'll be fine, Mom. Don't worry," she panted.

Between contractions she told herself that was true. This was a perfectly normal thing. Women had babies all the time. *Only it's different for me.* She tried not to think about the future, but it haunted her. *Why must I go through all this, the waiting and the pain, and yet never hold my baby in my arms?*

A few of the girls at Beulah Home did take their babies home, she knew. *But that wouldn't be fair.* She worried, not about her own shame—she could live with people talking about her behind her back—but about how people would talk about her child, calling it awful names.

She moaned, and her mother calmed her. "Hold my hand, Marianne. Hold it tight."

She had no way to support herself, and she couldn't ask her parents to share her burden. They'd all agreed it was best for her to give the baby up. The next contraction was the strongest yet. "Mama," she groaned as she gripped Carrie's hand.

Yes, they had all agreed, Mom, Dad, and Marianne. Major Hudson had promised the Salvation Army would find a good Christian home for her baby, but she would never see it. "It's easier that way," they had all told her.

The doctor came in and sent Carrie away. "She's doing just fine," he said. "It's time to take her to the delivery room."

The pain became worse, and while Marianne cried out, still, for her mother, she had to endure this alone. Well, not quite alone, she realized.

The nurse, dressed in white but with the familiar braid of the Salvation Army on her collar, spoke gently to her. "Just a little longer, Marianne. It will all be over very soon. Your baby's almost here."

One more terrible spasm, and one more scream. Then Marianne heard another cry, loud, lusty, almost angry, she thought. The doctor spoke softly to the nurse, but

Marianne felt a tremendous joy when she heard him. "It's a girl, a beautiful baby girl."

Marianne was exhausted, even though she'd slept for hours. As she woke, she saw her mother standing by a window, watching a late March rainfall. Marianne didn't call to her right away. She wanted to pray first, to thank God that her baby was healthy, and to plea for the little girl with an agony in her soul as great as the physical pain of giving birth. "Oh, God," she murmured, "please look after her. Find her a home, and a father, and a new mother who will love her as much as I do and will take good care of her and will teach her about your love. Please, God, please."

She must have spoken the last words aloud, because Carrie turned and hurried to her. "Everything's fine, honey. You just need a few weeks to get your strength back and then you can go home and forget this."

"How can I forget, Mama?" Marianne wondered how she could possibly feel so happy and yet so sad at the same time. "The doctor said it was a little girl." She sighed. "Did you see her?"

Carrie shook her head. "I wanted to, but I thought it was better if I didn't. Marianne, I guess I shouldn't tell you to forget about her. You never could. You'll always remember her and pray for her. But you have to get on with your own life now and trust God to protect his little one."

"Mama, I want to see her so much. I want to hold her, just once."

"They say it's better this way, Marianne. They say it's even harder afterward."

"It couldn't be any harder. She's been next to my heart for so long. I miss her so, Mama. I miss her so much already."

Carrie's eyes watered. "I'm sure these people know best. They want to make this easier for you, to help you do what you have to do."

"I know I have to give her up, Mama. I know I can't take care of her by myself, and it wouldn't be right for her if I tried."

"That's right." Carrie repeated the words Marianne had heard so many times in the past few months, "The best thing for the baby and for you is to give it up for adoption. The Salvation Army will see that it has a good, God-fearing mother and father."

"I know what I have to do, and I truly pray that God will give me the strength to do it. Mama, if they won't let me see her, at least you go. Just whisper to her that her mother loves her."

"Babies don't understand." Carrie blinked back her tears. "She won't know."

"Maybe not, but I will," Marianne insisted. "And then you can tell me she's all right. And someday, maybe, you can tell me about her—what color her hair is and her eyes."

"All babies have blue eyes, and all Hanlons have red hair too." Carrie tried to laugh. "Even most of the McLeans have red hair."

"Please, Mom. I just know, in my heart, no matter what anyone says, that she needs somebody to hold her and love her."

The Salvation Army lawyer would arrive soon with the papers for Marianne and Carrie, as her guardian, to sign. "I'll come back up in just a little while, Marianne, and take you home," Carrie promised.

"Thank you for going to see her, Mama. She is pretty, isn't she?" Marianne pressed. "She's pretty and healthy, and someone nice will want her?"

"She's perfect," Carrie assured her daughter. "Everyone who sees her will want her."

"I guess that's why you won't let me see her, then." Marianne's arms still ached to hold the little girl, but she struggled to hold back her tears. Carrie, too, looked heartsick, and Marianne tried to cheer her mother. "I'll be home soon, and I do so want to see Dad and Anna and Adele. I even miss Ted and Lizzie." She laughed gamely.

"Would you believe Liz told me the other day that she was tired of having a bedroom all to herself?"

"She'd better not be too unhappy about it. In a couple of years I'll be off to nursing school, and then to officer's training."

"Do you still mean to become a Salvationist, Marianne?"

"More than ever, Mama. They've been so good to me. I'd enlist right now, but they think I should wait until I'm older, and 'sure of my calling.'"

"They're good people," Carrie conceded. "And I'd be proud of you. But it's a hard life. I wanted so much for you to have the girlhood I didn't have—fun, parties, beaus."

"I guess the Lord had different plans, Mama." Marianne thought, again, of the child she'd never see. "Oh, how I wish I could make plans for her," she sighed. "Even if the Lord had other plans, if I could only have her for a little while."

Carrie took her daughter's hand. "I do understand, Marianne. Even if you should become a missionary I won't be losing you. Even if God and the Salvation Army send you far away, you'll write and visit. And I've had so much already. Marianne, I'm so very proud of you. You've been so brave, and you're so brave now, to give up that precious child."

"No I'm not, Mama. If I were brave I'd be happy for her. But I'm not. I'm selfish. I want to see her now, and I want to see her grow up."

"She's so beautiful." Carrie spoke almost to herself. "Everyone's child, blonde, blue eyed. She reached out to me. Oh, she didn't really, of course. She's much too little."

Marianne had caught her breath sharply, and Carrie put her hand over her mouth. "Oh, honey, I'm sorry. I shouldn't have said that. I didn't mean to."

"Everybody's child, but nobody's. Mama, no one could love her the way we do. I know what 'everybody' says, but how can it be right to trust her to strangers?"

Major Hudson came in then, with a man she introduced as Mr. Jacobson, a lawyer. Marianne picked up the pen to sign, as she had promised, but Carrie reached out and took it from her. "Could you wait outside for a few minutes?" she said to the major and the lawyer. "Maybe there is another way."

As they closed the door behind them, Marianne looked inquiringly at her mother. "But how? We've talked and talked and . . ."

"They told us we shouldn't see her, Marianne, and they were right, so right. And I told you anyone who saw her would want her."

"I know, but it just isn't to be." Marianne, just for a moment, felt as if she were the older. "How can we do anything else?"

"Marianne, your father and I could take her. I've been thinking about it, but I didn't say anything, because I didn't want to get your hopes up."

Hope. The word resounded in Marianne's heart as her mother continued.

"You're supposed to be in a sanatorium with TB. We could say the baby belonged to a friend of yours, who died. She . . ."

Carrie paused, and Marianne eagerly picked up the story. "She wanted her little girl to have the best possible home, so she asked you to take care of her."

"I'm sure your father would agree, Marianne. And we'd know, all of us, that she was well cared for. It's so obvious. Could you do it, honey? Could you go home and pretend she was your little sister?"

"Could I do anything else? Oh, Mama, you know it's the answer to all my prayers."

Both Major Hudson and the lawyer counseled against a spur of the moment decision. Carrie returned to Soledad, but a week later she and Matt came to Oakland together. After agreeing that appearances might best be served by Marianne staying in Oakland to finish the

111

school year, Carrie and Matt took little Ellen back with them to Soledad where, if anyone had any suspicions about the chubby blonde baby, they kept them to themselves.

Chapter Twelve

The train chugged up the grade south of San Jose. Live oak trees clung to the bits of soil hidden among the granite boulders. Soon the train reached the crest and began the descent into the Salinas Valley. This was the dividing line between Marianne's two worlds. She looked ahead. The valley had changed almost as much as she had. *Almost.*

She hadn't spent much time in the Salinas Valley during the past five years. There had been only a few short vacations from nursing school. Then she had worked for a year in San Francisco, before the grueling nine months of officer training school. She would enjoy being home, for a little while at least.

She had gone back to Soledad the June after Ellen's birth. The family and the people of Fort Romie said they were pleased that she'd recovered so completely from the tuberculosis they'd been told had sent her away. Adele, the only one other than Mom and Dad who knew the truth, had hugged her close and said only, "Welcome home, Marianne."

Thanks to the classes she'd taken at Beulah Home, and to Adele's tutoring, she did join the senior class at Gonzales High that fall, but it wasn't the same. Her classmates seemed distant, somehow, though she'd known most of them all her life. George, who had graduated now, was going with a girl from Gonzales; Marianne realized she felt relieved.

Ernie and Adele were considered a pair, but Adele soon confided to Marianne that "we're not a bit serious. Ernie never had a serious bone in his head anyhow." She giggled. "Marianne, I've been talking to Mama, and to Nancy. I think I want to go to normal school."

"You, a teacher! Adele, a classroom full of kids would drive you crazy," Marianne insisted.

"Oh, I don't know. Besides . . ." Adele leaned over and whispered confidentially, though the girls were alone at the time. "Think of the great men I could meet in San Jose."

Adele's laugh was infectious. Marianne might feel uncertain with her old friends, but with her family she was safe. And there was Ellen. The chubby blonde baby might as well have had two mothers, Anna had said once, since Marianne spent so much time caring for her.

Marianne had worked a little in the hospital ward at Beulah Home and felt more determined than ever to become a nurse. She studied hard that year, and between her books and the baby she kept so busy that she cared nothing for the social life Adele kept pushing on her.

She recalled the hayride. She wished she could laugh it off, but even now it didn't seem a bit funny. It happened after the first basketball game, with the first real chill of winter in the air. Adele had suggested borrowing the old hay wagon and team instead of taking the McLeans' truck to Gonzales, and she'd persuaded Marianne to go along. "You aren't going to turn into a recluse. I won't let you," Adele had insisted.

Marianne had enjoyed herself, she realized, as she snuggled down in the sweet-smelling wheat straw. Gonzales had beaten arch-rival King City, and everyone was in a great mood. The new boy, Tom, had been attentive, but not too attentive, on the ride up. Now, on the way home, Joannie snickered as Bill burrowed into the straw next to her; Adele urged Ernie to start a song, and as the half-dozen others joined in, Marianne slipped deeper into a corner of the wagon.

If the boys who'd known her before seemed to avoid her, Marianne hadn't noticed. Tom had come to Soledad just that summer. He was in a few of her classes, and he'd been nice enough. But now she heard the straw rustle as he edged in beside her. She tried to ignore his closeness, and he must have taken her quietness as permission. She felt his hand on her knee.

Everyone in the wagon heard the slap, and several of them exchanged amused glances. But only Marianne heard Tom's muttered snarl. "Why you, you little . . . Who do you think you are, anyhow? I'm not good enough for you?"

They rode the rest of the way back to Soledad in silence. *Just what has he heard?* Marianne wondered. *Does everyone in town think I'm a bad girl?* But after that she tried harder to treat Ellen as no more than a much-loved baby sister, and she dug even deeper into her books.

When she was accepted into the nursing school in San Jose the next summer, she was doubly glad. Not only was she on the way to fulfilling her dream, but she was escaping the gossip she never heard but never ceased to feel. *Surely,* she assured herself, *it will have ended by the time Ellen is old enough to hear it, especially if I go away.*

She knew no one in San Jose except Adele, who was much too busy with her studies and her social life to spend much time with Marianne. It didn't matter.

The three years had flown by, including the first year when she'd washed bedpans and wrapped bandages for hours on end. The next year she'd bathed patients, dressed wounds, and given medicine. While her fellow students grumbled at the long hours and lack of appreciation, she reveled in the responsibility and in the gratitude of the few patients who bothered to express it. "Why are we here," she asked her fellow students, "if not to be helpful in any way we can?"

It was during the last year of her training, though, that a whole new world opened up for Marianne. For one thing, she showed a special aptitude for obstetrics. Though unlicensed, Marianne became a capable emergency midwife. But if that weren't miracle enough, she was awed by the wonders of healing that she saw as she learned to assist in surgery.

Surgery . . . That was how she'd first met Paul. No, she wouldn't think about Paul. The Salvation Army— that was her life now.

She had joined the Salvation Army while she was in nursing school and applied for officer training as soon as she was capped. But the Army advised her to wait. She worked for over a year in a San Francisco hospital and proved herself a devoted soldier with the local Corps. She'd been happy there, especially after she met Paul.

There he was, again, in her mind, as he was always in her heart. She pushed aside his face and his voice. *Jade; I'll think about Jade.*

Marianne had written to Jade after she went back to Soledad, and Jade, who found few people willing to befriend a Chinese in California, had answered. Their friendship grew stronger as both girls matured. Jade had stayed on at Beulah Home working for her room and board while she earned a high school diploma. When the new and larger Booth Memorial Home had opened, she'd been put in charge of the nursery.

A few days after Marianne had learned she had been accepted for officer training, a happy letter had come from her friend. "Isn't it wonderful?" Jade had written. "I've been accepted too. We'll be classmates!"

And now I am getting ready to go to China, Marianne told herself. She sighed, deeply. *But with Jade, not with Paul.*

She had met him last July, just a year ago, while she was working in San Francisco. Captain Dr. Paul Cameron was a Salvation Army officer, too, and had come to San Francisco General as a Surgical Resident.

Marianne dabbed at her moist eyes as she tried not to remember Paul. *Oh, God*, she prayed silently. *Help me to be content with the life you've given me. Mom and Dad have loved me and supported me with all their heart; I have good, dear friends, like Jade, in the Salvation Army. I have work to do for you, and I know you love me and care for me. Why do I want more?*

But Paul's face wouldn't go away. Sometimes she remembered the face she'd seen last: somber, sharply cleft chin, uptilted black brows furrowed above frosty eyes that avoided her own, the slight flush of anger on his cheeks. More often, though, she saw the laughing face she'd seen that first morning in surgery. That laugh—how it had annoyed her at first.

Marianne had already heard gossip about the new surgeon, fresh from his internship back east. Now, scrubbed, masked, and gowned, she found herself standing next to Captain Dr. Paul Cameron. *Yes*, she thought, *he is as handsome as they said.*

He was very tall, so tall his shoulders slumped slightly as he leaned over the woman on the operating table. His long, delicate fingers wielded the scalpel Marianne had handed him, but he seemed to pay little attention to what he was doing. True, his strokes were firm and precise. The sponges he placed controlled the bleeding from the capillaries, and he deftly avoided larger veins and arteries as he opened the woman's abdomen. But . . .

"Has anybody seen the new Harold Lloyd flick?" he asked. *Really*, Marianne thought, *talking about moving picture comedies in surgery!* "Saw it last night," he continued. "It sure is a kick."

"I'm a Chaplin nut myself," the assisting intern responded hesitantly.

"Well, now," Paul drawled. "Have you seen *The Gold Rush* yet?"

Marianne noted, however, that his fingers never made a misstep, in spite of the guffaws that his surgical mask barely muffled. And, as the woman's abdominal cavity lay open, revealing a grapefruit-sized tumor, he dropped the conversation and began to concentrate on the surgery.

She tried, as she had been taught, to anticipate his needs. When he asked for a clamp, she had it in her hand already. When he had cut away the ugly mass and began to remove the sponges, she handed him sterile forceps without being asked. She finally began to relax, realizing the operation was nearly over. *That wasn't so bad,* she told herself. *I can't see that Dr. Cameron's so hard to work with.*

"Nurse!" he roared, and she jumped. "A towel, for my forehead. I don't want salt in this wound. Besides, I'm not sure my sweat's sterile."

The surgical needle she'd just threaded fell from her grasp to the floor. She picked up a towel and wiped the doctor's damp brow. Already his hand was extended for the suture. She always had several needles threaded and ready, and she handed one to him with scarcely a second's hesitation.

She was flushed as she removed her surgical gloves and mask in the scrub room. *I should have seen that he needed the towel,* she told herself.

"Hey, Red, not bad." His mask hung loose beneath his sharply cleft chin, and his wide grin showed off teeth perhaps a trifle large, but white and even. "I heard you were good." His ice-blue eyes danced. "Next time I'll let you close."

She knew he was teasing, of course. Later, at the nurses' home, she'd mentioned the encounter to some of the other nurses. "How could he be so casual?" she'd wondered aloud. "How can he tell jokes and laugh about Charlie Chaplin while he's operating?"

"They say he's awfully good," Fran, a Salvationist friend had commented. "And I've heard he knows it too."

"But he's sure one good-looking hunk of a man," Ginny, who was not a Salvationist, had added. "He'd sure be a great catch if he were available to us heathens." She snickered. "Of course, you're one of them, too, so I guess he is available to you."

"Me?" Marianne shook her head. She joined the banter of the other girls, but her soul still bore a scar. *Will I ever, ever share their dreams?* She had almost stopped hoping, but now she remembered the broad grin and the gentle jest. Paul was, as Ginny had put it, a great catch.

He was tall, a good head taller than she, and Marianne had always been the tallest girl in her class. His eyes were blue and his skin fair. His hair, in striking contrast, was coal black. He wore it parted in the middle and slicked down, but a stubborn wave persisted. "He'd never notice me," she insisted to the other nurses.

It was just coincidence, she assured herself, but her surgical assignments seemed to match his more often than not the rest of the summer. And she wasn't the only one who noticed. "I'm glad it's you and not me," Ginny had remarked as summer drew to an end. "That's one reason I'm sorry you're leaving. Dear Dr. Cameron is such a fussbudget I'd just as soon not work with him too often."

"Why, what do you mean, Ginny?" Marianne inquired. "Sure, he expects us to be on our toes, but . . ."

"I don't relish being bawled out in front of everybody because I accidently gave him a number 9 clamp when he wanted a number 8. Does he think everybody's as perfect as he is?"

"No, but they'd better be if they expect to be on *his* surgical team," Fran snickered.

"I still don't think he asks any more of us than he does of himself," Marianne defended. "After all, we're dealing with life and death. We do have to be perfect, or as close to it as humanly possible."

"Sure, sure," Ginny granted grudgingly. "But I'm only human, and Fran's only human. So I guess you and the noble Dr. Paul Cameron deserve each other."

"Oh, come on," Fran soothed. "Lighten up. None of us is perfect, but Marianne's right. We all try." She nudged Marianne with her elbow. "I think he did ask for you," she whispered, "and I think it's great."

Chapter Thirteen

*H*e wasn't even discreet, Marianne recalled, smiling at the memory. He kept turning up wherever she was in the hospital—accidently, of course. Well, he was a surgeon, and she was working on the surgical ward, and maybe it made sense for him to check incisions while she happened to be dressing them. But for some reason she saw much less of the other surgeons than of Paul Cameron.

He still told jokes in the operating room, but his hands never faltered, and the interns and nurses who worked with him seemed more relaxed, despite his demands, than they were with other surgeons. He kept his team on their toes, but he pulled patients through who might have died with other surgeons.

He knew when Marianne took her lunch break and usually found his way to the staff dining room at the same time. "Hi, Red," he'd opened the first time, with a wave of that long, delicate hand. "Mind if I sit here?"

"Suit yourself, Captain Dr. Cameron. It's not my table." She tried to smile just enough to be respectful but not enough to encourage him. He was a Salvation Army officer, but she hadn't even given him permission to use her given name, let alone that ridiculous nickname. "By the way," she said, trying not to sound too standoffish. "My name's Hanlon, Marianne Hanlon."

"Marianne." He rolled the name with a slight Southern drawl. "I kind of like that."

She blushed, and he chuckled. "Red suits you better, though."

"How is Mrs. Andrus doing?" she asked, trying to turn the conversation toward something impersonal.

"Oh, the ovarian cyst. Not bad, in spite of my bad jokes. You know, Red, I've noticed you don't laugh at my jokes. No sense of humor?"

He stared at her with the very slightest upturn to his lips, and she thought he could see the hairs rising on the nape of her neck. "Doctor Cameron, it's just that I never thought of the operating room as a place for laughter."

He nodded, then, and the corners of his mouth turned serious. "Marianne, don't you know that sometimes we have to laugh to keep from crying?"

By September, when she left the hospital to start officer training school, she knew she was going to miss Paul. Then, in mid-October, he somehow found out which Corps she'd been assigned to for Sunday Meeting. One morning he suddenly appeared and embarrassed her by asking Jade to move over so he could take the seat next to Marianne. After that he turned up each Sunday, and,

when his hospital schedule permitted, at weeknight meetings too. He never asked to walk her back to her dorm.
He just did.

At first her heart had thumped from the fear she still
hadn't totally shaken. A part of her wanted to pull away
from the courteous hand on her elbow and run to catch
up with Jade. But another part of her was hungry for his
talk, and his touch.

And Paul, always a gentleman, didn't seek out dark
pathways. Almost as if he understood her fear, he found
places where they could be alone in crowds, where they
could talk intimately, surrounded by strangers. Gradually
her deep fear gave way to the excitement of young love.

"But everyone's talking," she had confided to Jade one
rainy afternoon in December. "I know they are, and it
makes me uncomfortable." She actually giggled.

"Real uncomfortable," Jade observed with a smile.
"Do you realize that's practically the first time I've ever
heard you sound like a girl, a young, happy girl? I like it."

"Oh, Jade, don't be silly. I'm not a giggly schoolgirl,
and no man is going to turn me into one. I'm twenty-two
years old."

"Oooh, so young as that," Jade teased. "You're so
serious all the time, I'd have thought you were at least
thirty."

"Yot're a fine one to talk, Jade. How often do you act
silly? And, by the way, just how old are you?"

"You know you can never guess a Chinese lady's age,"
Jade evaded. "I've never been young, anyhow."

That's certainly true, Marianne thought. Jade had let very little slip about herself. She had been born in south China, Marianne knew. During one of the endemic revolutions, when the family farm had been overrun and the crops destroyed, her family had fled to Shanghai. While there, they had sold their only daughter into slavery. Jade still kept the rest of her past a secret. Marianne didn't even know how she came to America.

"I know you've had a hard life." Marianne squeezed her friend's hand. "But that's all over. When we graduate I'm sure you'll be assigned somewhere where you might even meet some good Christian Chinese men."

Jade's response had surprised her. "No," she said firmly. "That life isn't meant for me."

Marianne had felt the same way for so long. Men had meant Eric, but now, since she'd met Paul, her heart was light. "Believe me, Jade, I do understand. But when I'm with Paul I feel like a girl. I know I can trust him." *Well, almost*, she told herself. *And if I do draw away when he touches me, well, he did say he admired my modesty.* "Jade," she continued, "the Lord will give you happiness one day."

"He has, Marianne. I am content just to be free to serve the Lord. But I'm so happy to see that you do know how to laugh after all, my dear friend."

Marianne's practical work assignment, at her request, was at a shelter for girls, and frequently she received calls from the hospital chaplain, or even from Paul, to come and counsel a young patient. That was how she'd met Angie Parker.

125

Angie had been brought to the hospital by her mother, Paul explained hurriedly. She had developed peritonitis after an abortion. Marianne had had only a few minutes to talk with the pain-wracked girl, just time enough to assure her of Jesus' love and his forgiveness, before the raging fever claimed her life.

The glass-topped double doors of the charity ward swung shut behind her, and Marianne glanced around the shabby little waiting room. The girl's mother, a small, gray-haired woman, slumped in a corner of the bare wooden bench. Marianne sighed. This was the hardest part—trying to console the ones who had to go on living.

"Mrs. Parker?" she whispered. When the woman raised her swollen face, Marianne slipped onto the bench beside her and covered the woman's folded hands with her slender palm. "Mrs. Parker, I'm so sorry."

It wasn't necessary to say anything else, not right away at least. What made Marianne so good at the difficult task was her willingness to be quiet, to sit beside the family and wait until they were ready to hear more.

Sometimes it was a long wait, but Mrs. Parker hadn't expected good news. "Why, Nurse? My Angie wasn't a bad girl, really she wasn't. Why did God punish her?"

Marianne realized that Paul was waiting for her across the room. Well, he'd just have to wait. "Mrs. Parker, sometimes it's terribly hard for us to understand God's ways, but he is a forgiving God. I don't think he was punishing Angie. He knew her heart. Maybe he took her to be with him to end her suffering."

Mrs. Parker stared at the clinically clean tile floor. "Maybe he's punishing me. Maybe if I'd been more for-

126

giving, she wouldn't have done what she did, and she'd still be alive."

Marianne patted the knotted fingers. "You mustn't blame yourself, either. You loved her. God knows that, and Angie knew it too."

"She came to us, to her father and me, and asked for help, and we turned her away. Her father insisted she had disgraced us. That's why she went to that man."

Marianne recalled the day her own father had suggested that an abortionist might be the answer to her situation. Thank God her mother had been there for her, or she and Ellen, like Angie and her aborted child, might be dead.

"Angie went to him because she was afraid, and she didn't know who to turn to. If only she'd come to us right away, to our shelter, instead of going to an abortionist." Marianne shook her head sadly. "We could have cared for her, and for her baby. But even now I'm certain God is comforting Angie, Mrs. Parker. And he will comfort you, too, for he is a God of love and of mercy. It may take time, but we will be praying for you, and God will help you."

The older woman shook her head. "Her father told her to get rid of the baby or get out of the house, and I let her go. I let her go, and now she's dead. And I have to go home and tell her father that he needn't worry anymore about Angie disgracing him," she said bitterly.

"Would you like me to go with you, Mrs. Parker? Maybe it would help."

"No!" Mrs, Parker spoke sharply. "No, he hates you Salvationists. Hypocrites, he always says. No, I have to do this myself."

127

"If you're sure . . . But I'd like to come and visit you in a few days. We do want to help." Marianne supported her gently as she rose to go home.

Paul was still waiting. "I'm going to stay with Mrs. Parker until her bus comes," Marianne explained, and Paul took Mrs. Parker's other arm as they went outside.

"I hate this," he said to Marianne after they'd put the still weeping Mrs. Parker on her bus. "That girl was so young. It's such a waste."

"And so needless. If she'd only come to us, Paul, to the shelter instead of to that butcher. We could have cared for her, found a home for her baby." *Maybe even,* she thought, *reconciled her to her father and reunited the family.* "Her father, her own father, told her to get rid of the baby or get out."

"It's an unforgiving world we live in, Marianne. I guess a good Christian family could have found a better way. Still, it does prove sin has its own rewards. The real answer is to win these girls to Christ before they get themselves in trouble."

"They don't always 'get themselves' in trouble," Marianne reminded him. "Sometimes they are innocent and are taken advantage of."

"Sometimes," he conceded. "Certainly our heavenly Father is willing to forgive, and we are not to judge. But you know the girl is rarely that innocent."

But sometimes she is, Marianne wanted to shout, but a deep dread held her back. "Do you really believe that these girls die from botched abortions because of their sin, Paul?" she asked meekly. "If that were true, wouldn't they all die? Wouldn't the girls who didn't have abortions die

128

in childbirth? You know that isn't the kind of God we worship."

"Of course not. If I didn't believe in a God of mercy I wouldn't be a Salvationist," he insisted. "But I'm a realist too. Of course, God forgives, when we repent, but that's entirely different from claiming it wasn't sin to begin with."

He is right, of course, she thought. *It was sin, and it did take two . . . No,* she told herself firmly. *It didn't always take two.* "Not always," she whispered.

He seemed not to have heard. "I love your idealism, Marianne. You've such a loving spirit." His hand found hers as they walked, and she tried to be unconscious of his gentle, casual touch. "But you're so innocent yourself."

She thought of the secret he didn't know. *I have to tell him,* she thought. *I have to tell him soon.*

He was still talking about her supposed innocence. "I do admire your devotion to these girls, Marianne, but they're from a world you've never had to contend with. Surely even you must admit that most of them knew what they were doing when they went astray. Good girls don't put themselves in positions where they can be taken advantage of. Good girls don't have 'unwanted' babies."

She felt a cold shiver. *I was trying to help my own uncle,* she wanted to protest. *I didn't even know what 'taking advantage' meant.* She brushed aside the momentary panic. *He loves me; he'll understand how it was.*

Paul glanced at his watch and squeezed her hand gently. "You'd better hurry. You'll be late to supper."

"You're so sober tonight," Jade remarked later, when they were alone. "The girl died, didn't she?"

"Yes. It was too late to do anything for her. Oh, why don't they come to us? Jade, that could have been me."

"But it wasn't, Marianne. The Lord had work for you to do."

"And he gave me parents who accepted me, even after what happened. That girl's father—her own father, Jade—sent her to her death."

Jade sighed and looked away. When she turned back, Marianne saw tears on her cheeks. "Fathers do what they feel they must, and daughters do as their fathers tell them, in China and in America. Be grateful, Marianne. Your father sent you to the Salvation Army."

"Jade?" Marianne thought about what Paul had said. *He'd never send a girl in need away to die, but he blamed Angie, even so.* "Jade, I need to talk to someone who knows about me."

Jade sat down on her bed and patted the mattress beside her. "I thought so. Marianne, you still feel guilty, don't you? Surely you know Jesus has forgiven anything you did."

"Jade, I know, in my mind anyhow, that there was nothing for him to forgive. I was a victim, Jade. I was raped." She paused, and Jade nodded understandingly. "Jade, I think I'm falling in love with Paul. I thought I'd never trust any man, ever, but Paul's so good and so gentle. But he always talks about how 'innocent' I am."

"And so you are, Marianne."

"But will Paul think so, once he knows about Ellen? Or will he only understand that I had a baby when I was sixteen years old with no husband? Oh, Jade, must I tell him?"

Jade's eyes gave her the answer she knew was right, though it wasn't the answer she wanted. "Jade, there was some gossip at home, I think. Not that anyone ever said anything to me, but I could tell by the way they acted. When I went home after Ellen was born, most of the boys avoided me. One of them, someone I hadn't known before, thought I was trash and treated me like it. The others, the ones I'd known all my life, well, mostly, they left me alone."

Jade nodded. "Gossip is a vicious thing, and someone was bound to be suspicious. It's human nature."

"I'm afraid something else is human nature, too, Jade. Men don't want spoiled goods. But I couldn't marry Paul without him knowing, could I? I mean, what if he found out later? No." She gazed out the window at a bright full moon. "Even if he didn't, I'd know. It would always be between us."

"I know Paul spends a lot of time with you, and, yes, I suspect he's falling in love with you, too, but has he mentioned marriage?"

"Not yet." Marianne paused for a moment. "There's no reason I can't be his friend without his knowing, is there? If I told him now, and he really didn't care, I'd only be making a fool of myself. Later, if he says anything . . ." She picked up her Bible and began to study the day's lesson. "If that time comes, surely he'll understand."

She couldn't concentrate. She thought of Paul's words, of how he thought of her as pure and innocent. *Innocence? What Paul means by that word was taken from me that evening at the mission, and I can never get it back. I'm not innocent.* Her cheeks burned, and tears slipped down to cool them. *But I am innocent,* her logical mind told her. *Innocence is the opposite of guilt, and I am not guilty, not of this.*

She slipped to her knees. How many times before had she tried to pray for God's forgiveness, yet never really found peace? She confessed other sins, and knew they were forgiven. But this . . . She had no new words, so she used no words. She wept, and she listened, and deep in her soul she heard Jesus' answer. At last she knew in her heart that she hadn't found forgiveness because there was nothing to forgive.

Chapter Fourteen

*M*arianne and Paul went to a
street meeting that night in
Chinatown. As had become his easy, quiet, yet deliriously
happy habit, he took her arm as the meeting ended and
steered her away from the others. Now they lingered over
a late supper in a little family cafe overlooking Grant
Avenue. "Delicious egg rolls." He handed her the plate.
"You do like Chinese food, don't you?"

"Mmmm? Oh, yes, I love it." She took one of the
crispy appetizers and nibbled on it. "I was looking at the
people down there on the street. Chinese going home;
San Franciscans out for dinner; tourists. Poor people,
working people, rich people. They're all in such a hurry.
I wonder where they're going."

"I prefer the view in here," he said, so softly she hardly
heard.

She sighed. "We've no right to be so happy, Paul.
There is so much need in the world. We have so much,
and they have so little."

"Don't feel too sorry for them. Most of the people strolling Grant Avenue on a Saturday night have a lot more money than a couple of Salvation Army officers will ever have."

"You know I don't mean that, Paul. Some of them do have more money, but so few of them have peace. In fact, I feel more sorry for the rich in a way."

He stared at her, puzzled. "Blessed are the poor, I guess, but what in the world are you getting at?"

"Well, poor people know they are needy; they aren't afraid to ask for help. But rich people don't seem to be able to admit their need. You know, like Jesus said about how hard it is for the rich man to get into heaven. Because the rich man doesn't think he needs anything, even God."

"Does that mean you think we should minister more to the rich, then?"

"No, I guess not." She finished the spicy egg roll. "But we shouldn't ignore them, either."

"Marianne, you couldn't ignore anyone if your life depended on it. But you do have a heart for the outcasts. I've watched you working with the girls from the shelter, and I know the Lord is using you there. Do you think that is the mission you've been called to?"

"Maybe," she responded. It was an opening, she realized. Perhaps now was the time to tell him why she identified so well with the girls she counseled, to tell him about Ellen. *But why? It can wait. If he really gets serious, if he mentions marriage, then I'll have to tell him. But,* she rationalized, *why risk losing his friendship now, when it isn't necessary?*

"I haven't thought much, really, about my 'mission' as you call it," she told him. "I'll go where I'm sent and accept my Army orders as God's will."

"Spoken like a good soldier." His lips curled into a half smile. "I grew up with that, and I never knew my parents to grumble, in public anyhow. Marianne, I love the Salvation Army. It's my family. But I'm still an individual, and I feel God has given me a burden for China."

"China?" She was startled. "You feel a burden for China? It's so far away and has so many wars. Yet since I've known Jade, I've felt the Lord might send me there too."

He stared at her, and a slow smile spread across his face. "You too?" he answered. "Truly the Lord works in mysterious ways," he added softly.

"There is so much need there," she explained, hoping he would know that her mention of China wasn't just idle flirtation.

"Yes, Marianne. There is such terrible need, for both medicine and the gospel."

"Jade's told me a little." She paused, but she trusted Paul enough to share Jade's story with him. "Did you know she was sold, was a slave, in Shanghai?"

"Oh, no! How sad. I knew only that she's your good friend and that she's Chinese, of course. That's why I brought up the subject. But I scarcely dared hope you might share my call."

"Actually, I've always had this feeling God wanted me to be a missionary, Paul, but then I met Jade." She paused, thoughtfully. "I suppose it has been the Lord's leading, but I like Jade, and she doesn't have many friends." She hesitated. "You know how it is here. White people don't have much to do with Chinese, and there are no other Chinese cadets this year. So she's alone."

"Yes. She seems very pleasant, but I know it's hard being different." He chuckled. "I was the Salvation Army kid in school. My parents were officers and that made for quite a bit of guff. Believe it or not, I can understand her feelings."

Marianne nodded. "I had it easy when I was little. I grew up on a farm, near a small town. Everybody knew everybody; everybody took care of everybody. But . . ." Again an inner voice told her that now was the time to tell him why she, too, was a loner. But her fear of rejection still held her back.

He took her hands in his across the table. "God has given you a great gift, Marianne. The psychologists call it empathy. You sensed Jade's loneliness and responded. You have compassion for the girls at the shelter and demonstrate God's forgiveness. You even recognize that young doctors may not be as confident as they appear and encourage them. Thank you."

She blushed at his words. If he knew why she understood, would he still think so well of her? But oh, how wonderfully his words warmed her.

The waiter brought more hot green tea and a small plate of fortune cookies. Paul slowly released her hands, and she missed the warmth of his touch. He handed her one of the sparkly sugar-glazed triangles, and broke open the other. "Your enterprise has an auspicious beginning," the slip of paper he laid on the table read. "So, what's your fortune?"

"Oh, you don't really believe these, do you?"

"Of course not." He looked down at the slip of paper. "But I hope this one's right. Now come on, what 'auspicious' message did you get?"

It was silly, she told herself once more. You didn't get messages from God in Chinese fortune cookies. She handed him the paper, knowing it would be, to him, just an old Chinese adage. "See no evil; hear no evil; speak no evil."

Marianne and Paul had been seeing each other three or four times a week all winter, but, she told herself, it was mostly at Salvation Army Meetings or at the hospital. She knew she loved him; she felt a completeness, a security in his presence and emptiness when they were apart. She reveled in being with him, and even as she tried to convince herself he wasn't courting her, she knew he cared as much as she did.

I should never have let it go this far, she worried. His parents were in town, and he was taking her to dinner with them. Would they approve of her? She could only hope so. Would they approve of her if they really knew her? She trembled, ever so slightly.

Major and Mrs. Major Cameron were being transferred from their post in Portland, Oregon, and had stopped in San Francisco for a visit with their son. "Mother's been sick a lot there," Paul had explained. "She's used to a drier climate, so they're going back to

Texas, where I grew up. You'll like them. Really, you will."

"But will they like me?"

He shook his head in feigned bewilderment. "My dear, sweet Red, what's not to like? They'll not only like you, they'll love you."

They're nothing like I thought they'd be, Marianne mused as the foursome made polite conversation over their frijoles and enchiladas in the little Mexican restaurant Paul had chosen. *He must have gotten his black hair from his father,* she thought, *but where did he get his height?*

The Major sat ramrod straight, but was certainly no taller than average, and his hair, which might have been dark once, was a very dignified white. Petite Mrs. Major Cameron was still quite pretty, in a sweet, motherly way, though her sandy brown hair was streaked with gray. *So typically Salvation Army,* Marianne couldn't help saying to herself, smiling at her own stereotype.

"The enchiladas are quite good, aren't they, Marianne?" Mrs. Cameron's smile was warm. "Of course, they make them a bit livelier down in San Antonio, but . . ."

Marianne was washing the peppery food down with great gulps of ice water. "Livelier?"

"I guess Marianne hasn't developed a taste for Mexican food yet, Mother," Paul offered. "I've been training her on Chinese instead."

"You still feel strongly that the Lord wants you in China, don't you, Paul?" His mother's gentle voice couldn't hide her regret, but the major drew himself up even straighter, proud of his son's ambition. Mrs. Major

Cameron turned to Marianne. "Do you hope to go to the mission field, too, my dear?"

"Why, yes," Marianne admitted. "I've always wanted to be a nurse, and I have thought of being a missionary. The Lord sent me a very dear friend who is Chinese and is teaching me a little of their language. So it does seem the Lord is leading me in that direction."

Mrs. Cameron smiled at her modest pause, as Paul jumped in, "With a little help from me, of course."

Major Cameron glanced from one young face to the other and nodded approvingly. "It's a noble vision. Of course we would hate to have our only son go so far from us, but if it is the Lord's will, we will send him off proudly."

"Of course we will," Mrs. Cameron agreed. "But we'll be proud of Paul no matter what path he follows. He's always been bright, and so kind, and so faithful."

"I haven't done that well," Paul demurred. "But I've had the best kind of example to follow." He turned to Marianne. "These two have everything I want in my own life. You'll never know two people who are more truly one in the Lord. They've always told me God's servants must be above reproach, but more than that, they've lived it."

"He's a bit prejudiced," the major responded. "But we've tried to serve the Lord faithfully, and I thank him both for his strength and for the helpmate he gave me." He patted his wife's hand tenderly.

Marianne's own hand trembled as Paul reached out and covered it with his. "Yes," his father was saying, "the best foundation for a fruitful ministry is a sound Christian home. If we cannot set a good example, how can the lost find the way?"

Paul's hand closed tightly on hers, and Marianne's heart skipped. He wanted between them the love and trust he saw between his own parents, and it was a dream she wanted, more than anything, to share. They seemed to like her, to approve of her, in fact. Now she felt certain he would ask her, soon, to be his wife. *Oh, God,* her heart cried out, *let him understand.*

Chapter Fifteen

Marianne knew, as any woman in love would know, that beneath Paul's apparently casual possessiveness lay as fervid a passion, and as firm a commitment, as her own. She had known, certainly since the dinner with his parents, that he would one day ask her to marry him. And she dreaded testing his love, as she knew she must, by telling him her secret.

Her commissioning was approaching. It was April, and it had been a warm spring day in San Francisco. As Marianne strolled with Paul through the park, a cool evening breeze caught at her bonnet, and she reached up to settle it sedately atop her thick hair.

"Are you cold?" Paul asked. "We can take a trolley if you'd rather."

"No," Marianne assured him. "We get so little chance to just walk and enjoy the flowers."

Passersby smiled. Except for the austere uniforms with their bright red SA emblem and Marianne's bonnet, they looked like any other young couple walking through the park in the twilight. Paul saw that Marianne was shivering, and impulsively put his arm around her shoulders.

"People will talk," she protested, but not very convincingly. New memories had shut out the old, and she was warmed by his touch. "They think we're not supposed to do that."

"Who cares what they think?" He smiled and his arm tightened around her. "Why shouldn't I hug my girl?"

"Your girl?" She tried to sound as casual as he, but Marianne's heart skipped at his words.

"Don't be coy," he teased. "Everybody else knows we're going to get married after you're commissioned. Even the Army's permission is only a formality."

"Oh, it is?" If only the necessity for Army permission was all that stood between them. She knew the time had come. She could stall no longer. She had to tell him.

But he was still speaking. "It is only a formality, isn't it? Marianne, you must know how much I've come to love you, and I believe you love me too. God has led us to each other. I know in my heart he means for us to serve him together." He put a slender hand under her chin and lifted her face so her eyes met his. "Marianne, you will marry me, won't you?"

She watched his eyes grow puzzled as she remained silent. "Marianne, you do love me. I know you do. So do say 'yes.'"

She wanted to look away, but his eyes, fearful now, held hers. "Paul, I do love you, but there is something you have to know."

"Secrets?" He sat down on a bench and gently pulled her to him. "What secrets could a girl like you have? What could you tell me that I don't already know?"

"It happened a long time ago, Paul, a lifetime ago." She stared down at her hands until he took them in his own. "In Soledad. I was only fifteen."

She felt his puzzled gaze and hurried on, anxious to have the secret out, to share it with this man she'd come to love. "Paul, it's about Ellen."

"Your little sister? But Marianne, what could you possibly have to tell me about your sister?" He stopped abruptly, and Marianne could imagine his thoughts. "I know she's adopted, but . . ."

"She isn't my sister, Paul. She's my daughter."

She felt his hands tighten quickly over hers, and then, just as quickly, the cool wind chilled her fingers as he drew his away. Though he didn't move away, she felt a distance grow between them as she went on. "Paul, I was only fifteen. I didn't know."

"Of course, you didn't." He took her hands again, but she no longer felt any warmth in his touch or his words. "And it was a long time ago. You were a girl then; now you're a woman."

He seemed to be talking more to himself than to her, Marianne thought, as he continued. "You're a fine, Christian woman, and whatever happened before you came to the Lord is forgiven."

He stood then and began to walk back toward the training school. Marianne followed. He'd completely misunderstood, she realized. He thought she'd been to blame. "That wasn't the way it was," she protested. "I was raped."

He didn't seem to have heard her. "It wasn't my fault, Paul, but you had to know. I couldn't marry you without your knowing."

He still didn't answer. *Why doesn't he say something?* "Please, Paul,"

He looked down at her, kindly, she thought. *Only kindness!*

"Paul, I'm sorry. I should have told you sooner, but no one knows except my mother and father. They did adopt Ellen, legally, and everyone at home thinks her mother was a friend of mine. Paul, I didn't want to hurt you."

"No. But you led me on and let me love you, let me build my dreams around you." He almost seemed to be throwing the words at her. "If you'd only told me sooner, before I'd come to love you. I do love you, Marianne. I want you, and I love you, and I know this shouldn't matter."

Shouldn't, he'd said, not *doesn't.* They walked on in silence until they were in front of the cadets' living quarters. "Marianne," he whispered as she turned to go inside. "Marianne, I do love you. But I need a little time, just a little time, to work through this."

A little time! Thank God she was kept so busy during those last weeks before commissioning that she scarcely had time to realize he avoided her. He came to Corps Meetings, but he didn't sit in the seat she left vacant for him. He didn't wait for her afterward, or offer his arm and steer her away from the group when they walked back from street preaching. He was civil; he was polite; and he was cold.

"Marianne, I don't want to pry, but something's happened between you and Paul hasn't it?" Jade asked one day, as she helped Marianne bathe the babies in the shelter's nursery. "Everyone thought you'd be announcing your engagement by now, but then, suddenly you seem to be avoiding each other."

"Things didn't work out," Marianne snapped. "It just wasn't God's will for us."

"Maybe not," her friend conceded. "But it sure looked like it for a while there. Marianne, you told him, didn't you?"

Marianne nodded. "Oh, he was kind, Jade. He said he knew it shouldn't make a difference, but it did."

"If he had loved you, Marianne . . . Oh, I know that sounds cruel. What can I say, when you're hurting so? But Marianne, God loves you. It will work out."

"I know that's true, Jade. I know it's God's will, but I thought Paul loved me, really loved me. And we had so much in common, so many shared dreams—like China."

She sighed, pinned the last diaper corner, and took the squirming newborn back to his bassinet. "I still believe the Lord wants me to go to China, though." She brought another baby to the basin Jade had just refilled.

"Have you heard anything definite yet?"

"No. You know marching orders seldom come until the last minute. But you say yourself that I'm doing well learning the language, and my heart is so burdened for the girls you've told me about there. It just seems logical that I'll go to China someday, even without Paul. Maybe you and I will be sent there together."

A shadow crossed Jade's usually serene face. "Maybe."

"Don't you want to go back and tell your own people about Jesus' love?"

"Of course I do," Jade said quickly. "There is so much need. But . . ."

"But you like living in America."

"That's not it, quite. Oh, of course life's much easier here, but what does that matter compared to what the Lord has done for me? And if I were to be sent back, I know Jesus would protect me."

"From the riots, you mean? I've heard there's been a revolution and trouble in some of the cities, but that just means the need is greater."

"There's always a revolution going on somewhere in China." Jade's mouth twisted up in a semblance of a smile, but drooped again immediately. "No, it isn't the riots, Marianne. Let's just say there are people there I'd rather not see again."

Marianne opened her mouth to ask another question, but Jade had carefully put her placid, tranquil face back on. "I'll go wherever I'm sent, and gladly, and I know you will too. Maybe they'll send us to China together, so you can continue your language lessons." She forced a smile again. "You could still use an interpreter."

"Thanks for the compliment." Marianne smiled. "And for helping with the baths," she added as Jade slipped out of her big rubber apron and turned to leave. Marianne tucked the last baby in, and her eyes lingered on the tiny face.

Paul was a good man and a forgiving one. He'd said he loved her, and she believed he had. But she'd been right all along. Her hopes for a normal life, a husband, children, had ended that day back in Soledad, after Tim and Nancy's wedding. If Paul, who loved her, couldn't accept her, who would? His father had been right; a Christian worker must be above reproach. And Paul himself had said once that it took two to commit that particular sin.

It wasn't fair, but, as she saw every day in the shelter, life wasn't fair. A man, in a moment of insane lust, could take a woman's virtue, and even God, who forgave, couldn't make her clean again in man's sight. She told the girls she counseled that Jesus would forgive them and that they must forgive themselves. But oh, how long it had taken her to follow her own advice.

But how can I say my life is ruined? she reflected. *I've got Ellen. Maybe she'll never call me Mama, but at least I can watch her grow up, and look out for her. And I must trust the Lord for the rest. If it is his will that I stay single to serve him better, I must learn to be content with that.*

The commissioning service took place on a Friday evening in June. As Marianne looked out at the friends and family gathered in the auditorium, she thought briefly of her own family, too far away to come and see her graduate but proud of her, supporting her decisions, even when they disagreed. Mom, Dad, and Jesus accepted her just as she was, she realized. They knew everything, and they loved her.

She'd spent almost a year with the cadets who were becoming Salvation Army Lieutenants that night, living in the same house with the other girls, eating with them, studying with them, working with them. They were her friends, but none of them except Jade really knew her.

She saw Paul. *This might be the last time I see him,* she thought. Briefly she considered what might have been, if she'd just kept her secret. *But do I really want a man who doesn't love me enough to understand?*

There was a reception after the ceremony, but Marianne slipped away as soon as she could and went outside. She was surprised by a touch on her shoulder, and turned to see Paul beside her. "May I have a minute, Marianne? I think we should talk."

Maybe there is still a chance, she thought wildly. If he could just say that he didn't care, that he still wanted her. Her old dream surfaced: he, the tall, trim, stalwart soldier; she, the willing helpmate, off to do battle together and win the victory for the Lord. And babies she could claim openly, babies who would call her mother.

"Marianne, I know I've treated you terribly these past weeks. Believe me, I'm sorry. I know I've hurt you."

"I'd hurt you too," she told him, trying not to hope.

"It was the shock, I guess. I'd come to care for you very much, too much. To me you seemed to be everything a woman should be, pure, innocent."

Seemed? Her hope receded as he continued.

"Marianne, it isn't your fault. It's mine."

But what had he done except recoil from her shame? "It's not your fault, or mine," she told him. "What happened, happened."

148

"I have forgiven you, really I have."

Forgiven me, she thought. *But he still blames me.* Her hope was nearly gone.

"Marianne. I loved you. God help me, I still do. And I'm trying to forget what happened before."

A part of her longed to plead her case, but Marianne knew he had already judged her. He was still talking. *Why? What more could he say.*

"Forgetting is the hard part, Marianne," he went on. "I love you, but when I look at you, all I can think is that there has been someone else. Maybe, in time, I can forget, but I have to be as honest with you as you have been with me. I want to marry you, but I can't."

His eyes avoided hers. "I'm sorry. Please forgive me, Marianne."

He was asking of her what he admitted he couldn't give. He wanted her forgiveness, but he couldn't forgive her. *If he doesn't love me enough even to listen to me, does he love me enough to be my husband? And do I love him enough to care?* But the ache in her heart told her the answer to the question she'd asked herself. She did love him; she did care.

"I have my orders," he told her flatly. "I'm sailing for China next week—to a group of dispensaries, in the interior. There's war there now. It wouldn't be a safe place for a woman anyhow. Perhaps, someday . . ."

Feeling totally alone, she went back to the dorm. He was going to China, but she wasn't going with him. On her way to her room she found an envelope in her mailbox. She lifted her chin, squared her shoulders, and opened her own orders.

Chapter Sixteen

*M*arianne's train stopped briefly at the Salinas depot, and she studied the valley and its changes. Fields that would have been green with sugar beets five years ago were pale green now—lettuce green. Her cousin Harry had been experimenting with truck crops in high school only seven years ago, and now everyone in the valley was growing lettuce. Packed with ice and shipped in the new refrigerated freight cars, Salinas Valley lettuce had already become famous not only in California, but all over the United States as well.

June was a wonderful time in the Salinas Valley, Marianne mused. The rains were over and the sun shown every day. A gentle breeze blew up the river from Monterey Bay every afternoon. The summer cycle of morning and evening fog would set in soon, and everyone would be grateful for it, despite the gloom, because lettuce thrived in the cool dampness, and lettuce was what mattered in Soledad now.

Marianne had read in the newspaper about the collapse of wheat prices and sugar beet prices. Navy beans weren't even mentioned anymore, though the Hanlons' prosperity had been built on them during the war. There were droughts in the Midwest, and farmers all over the country were losing their mortgaged land to the banks that had so eagerly extended credit back in 1917 and 1918.

But while farmers felt the pinch, city people experienced such prosperity as they'd never seen before. Factories turned out everything from corn flakes to automobiles. Henry Ford, way off in Detroit, was paying $5 a day to the men who built Model Ts, so they could afford to drive them.

In the Salinas Valley, most of the farmers had turned to the new crops, crops the city people wanted and would pay for even when they were out of season and had to be shipped across country.

There they are! As the train pulled up to the platform Marianne saw her father and mother waiting. And Ellen! Ellen was just six years old, still chubby, still blonde and blue eyed. Marianne's heart leaped as she watched the little girl jump up and down eagerly, restrained only by Carrie's firm grip on the strings of her wide blue sash.

Restrained. I must be restrained too, Marianne thought, as she reached for the overnight bag in the overhead rack. *Mom and Dad first. I mustn't be overeager to kneel down and hug that precious little girl. I wonder if there's still gossip. Please, God.* It was the same silent prayer she'd prayed every day for six years. *Please God, protect my child.*

Carrie hugged her daughter warmly, then pushed her away a little and looked at her proudly. "The uniform becomes you." She grinned. "But try to lose the bonnet."

"Oh, Mom." Marianne turned to her father and kissed him affectionately on the cheek.

"Mi'anne, Mi'anne," she heard. The girl tugged at her skirt, and Marianne bent, eagerly, so the plump arms could circle her neck.

Ellen had seen Marianne only occasionally during her six years. *Surely she doesn't remember me,* Marianne thought. But then, Carrie would never have let her forget.

"Since your train was due in so late, we thought you'd rather go straight home and get some rest tonight, Marianne," Carrie said as Marianne stood up with Ellen's hand clasped tightly in her own. "Anyhow, it's past Ellen's bedtime already."

"Lizzie and Ted didn't come with you?"

"They wanted to, but we figured with the four of us and all your baggage, the car would be too crowded," Matt explained. "They're waiting at home, and I expect that'll be the end of your mother's idea of getting you to bed early. But don't let them pester you to death. You've got two whole weeks to answer all their questions."

"I've got so much catching up to do," Marianne said, as she got into the backseat of the new Chevrolet sedan her father had bought to replace the Studebaker. Ellen climbed in beside her, and she gave the child another hug. "And we have to get acquainted, don't we?" she whispered.

"Everybody's anxious to see you," Carrie said, turning around in the front seat and smiling at her daughters. "I hope you don't mind that I've invited Anna, Will and Irene, and Tim and Nancy over for supper tomorrow night."

"And all the kids." Matt laughed, and Carrie nodded. "Think you can keep all of the youngest generation straight?"

"I've never even seen half of them." It was Marianne's turn to laugh. "Let's see, I know Sammy, and then there's Joey—he was born while I was still here, and Beth." She listed them all, to refresh her memory. "Tim and Nancy had Johnny just about the time Ellen was born, then Kitty, and now Peter's the baby. See, Mom, I do read your letters."

Marianne's eyes searched out the familiar farmhouse in the shade of the old willows. The sun had nearly set, and the pale half-moon had begun to rise. Marianne saw the evening star next to it and suppressed the romantic wish that flashed through her mind. But she did wish, without forming the words, that Paul were with her, meeting these people she loved as much as she loved him.

Liz and Ted were waiting on the porch. "Mom let me redecorate our old room, Marianne." Liz bubbled with the joy of being suddenly grown up, now that she'd finished high school and had a job—a real job, she gushed—at the bank in Soledad.

Ted took the heavier of her two bags, Marianne noticed, and their father followed up the stairs with the lighter. Ted was just back from his second year of college, way up in Davis, near Sacramento. "Can you imagine?" Dad had said proudly. "Matt Hanlon's son going away to the University of California to learn to be a better farmer than his old man ever hoped to be."

The next morning, as she sat in her mother's kitchen, Marianne looked out across fields that had always sprouted wheat or sugar beets or beans. Now she saw the pale green of acre upon acre of lettuce. Here and there she spotted slightly darker gray-green patches of cabbages and bright, feathery squares of carrot tops.

Across the lettuce fields to the west she watched as migrant workers bent low over another new crop. Matt had planted some strawberries a year ago. Now they were picking the first harvest, which ripened just quickly enough, but not too quickly, in the gentle sun.

In her light cotton housedress, Marianne felt almost undressed after so much time in either her starched white nurse's uniform or the heavy navy blue Salvation Army uniform she always wore in public.

The farmhouse kitchen that had seemed so huge when she was a girl felt strangely small compared to the one in which she'd helped prepare meals at the training school. Yet it seemed empty, too, with only Marianne and her mother working in it. Marianne shelled peas from her mother's kitchen garden while Carrie pounded flour-coated steaks for the swiss steak she planned to serve that night.

"Is Adele coming to supper?" Marianne asked. "You didn't mention her, and I know she's awfully busy right now, but I was hoping to meet the lucky man before the wedding."

154

"No, they couldn't come tonight. Donald has a School Board meeting," Carrie answered. "Word is that he'll be the new principal next year."

"Hey, good for him." Marianne was happy for Adele. Not only had she discovered a real aptitude for teaching while she was in San Jose, but she'd also met Donald. He was from Oakland, but he had followed Adele back to the valley and taken a job at Salinas High School. "Principal, after only two years. How wonderful for both of them."

"Yes, Adele's deliriously happy. She's bringing him over to show him off to you tomorrow evening." Carrie's smile faded. "Marianne, I'm so proud of you. But I want you to be happy too. When I think what Adele has to look forward to, and then picture you halfway around the world, alone, it breaks my heart."

"Mom, you know happiness doesn't depend on marrying a successful man and having a nice house in town. I know I'll be happy in China, if I ever get there, because I'll be where Jesus wants me, serving him."

"Maybe if you were married and going with your husband, I wouldn't be so afraid for you, Marianne. I know being married isn't everything. Having a husband can't solve all the problems, and I wouldn't for anything want to see you married just to be married." Carrie pounded her steak firmly. "Well, at least you're not going right away. Maybe something will happen in the meantime."

"I asked to be sent to China, Mother. I guess it started when I met Jade and got to know her. It's so sad there, especially for the girls. They say that in Shanghai, where Jade comes from, one house in twelve is a brothel! Little girls, eight or ten years old are sold into them."

Carrie winced. "It's horrible, of course. But what can one or two young women do? It's their way of life. Those people don't know anything else."

"'Those people' as you call them, are God's creatures too. One or two young women can tell a few of them about Jesus and his love. And some of them do run away, or are thrown out when they, well, when they become less desirable. So one or two women can take them in, give them a home, teach them to read and write and to earn an honest living. Besides, it probably won't be just the two of us. They already have some clinics in cities in the north. And if they send us to a new place, like Shanghai, where Jade is from, I'm sure they'll send a married couple too."

"It just isn't fair, Marianne."

"Life's not fair. Maybe here you don't see that. You plant your crops, fertilize them, cultivate them, harvest them, and sell them. And you'll have a nice house, and your daughters will marry well, and your sons will prosper. But out there, in other parts of the world, it isn't like that. I see them, Mom, every day, over and over."

"I know why you feel the way you do. But just because you were an innocent victim doesn't mean there aren't a lot of people who bring their troubles on themselves. How many of those girls you feel so sorry for are really innocent victims?"

"Does it matter how many? Does blame matter at all?" She felt a stab of pain as she thought of Paul. She knew she wasn't to blame, but that hadn't mattered to him.

"Some of them were innocent," she continued, "and some weren't. Of the ones who weren't, well, some of them do go back and do the same thing over again. But, Mama, we can't turn our backs on all of them because we fail with some. We have to love them all, because Jesus loves them. And some of them do find him and build new lives, good lives. We have to keep trying."

"Is that why your noble doctor abandoned you to go off to save the heathens—are they more forgivable because they're Chinese?" Carrie bit her lip. "I'm sorry. I shouldn't have said that. Bitterness doesn't help."

"He didn't abandon me, Mom. We weren't married or even engaged."

"But you told him, and he turned away. Isn't that what happened?"

"It was God's will." It didn't really take away the hurt, but she knew the truth of what she said, even though it sounded so trite. "Mom, I won't say it didn't hurt. There is an empty space in my heart that may never be filled. But I do know, from experience, that God does heal our pain eventually. And our hurt does help us to help others. You know that I would never have come to this point if what happened hadn't."

"I do know that, and I'd give anything if it could be undone. But maybe you shouldn't have told Paul. It's hard for a man to understand. It's natural for him to want to be the first with his wife." She paused and shook her head thoughtfully. "Maybe it's selfish, rather than honest, to put that burden on a man."

"You didn't believe that before I told him about Ellen. You agreed, then, that he had to know. You haven't changed your mind, have you?"

"I guess not," Carrie admitted. "But why did he turn away? You did explain how it was, how Eric took advantage of you, didn't you?"

"I told him, Mama, but all he heard was that I had a child. Nothing mattered after that."

"If he truly loved you, how could he blame you?"

"A man blames a woman. Sure, it's wrong, but that's just the way it is," she said sadly. "Mama, don't be too hard on Paul. I truly believe he wanted to marry me. But he expected his wife to be pure. He just couldn't put that aside."

Chapter Seventeen

*T*im and Nancy were the first to arrive for the family supper Carrie had promised. "Wow, a Packard," Marianne whistled. "The dairy business must be very good indeed."

Even the kids were smartly dressed. Johnny's knickers were topped by a white shirt and jaunty bow tie, and Kitty wore a starched and ruffled pinafore and patent leather pumps. Nancy's slim short silk sheath was belted stylishly at her hips. Tim, actually wearing a suit, grinned as he hoisted year-old Peter onto his shoulder. "Yup, couldn't be better. You knew I sold the creamery, didn't you?"

"Mom did write something about it," Marianne told him. "But you still have the dairy herd?"

"Milking over a hundred head," he told her proudly. "All done with milking machines now. And we're breeding stock for sale too. Got a Grand Champion Holstein bull in fact."

"You always have liked livestock," Carrie interrupted.

"Yes, he has," Nancy agreed. As Johnny and Kitty dashed off to join Ellen on the swing Matt had hung from one of the willow trees, she called, "Be careful not to spoil your clothes." She turned to Marianne. "My, you look swell. I just can't believe you're still single, with that figure and that gorgeous red hair."

Will's arrival with Irene and their children covered the awkward moment. Unlike his brother, Will wore jeans and a denim work shirt, and he still drove his old Chevy. Irene had put on some weight, Marianne noted, and her clothes were less stylish. They both had the calloused hands of farmers.

Tim greeted his brother. "How's the deal coming with Rutherford?"

"Will's trying to buy another farm," Nancy explained to Marianne. "He's positively land crazy, that Will. Just look. You'd think they were dirt poor the way Irene dresses and everything, but they'll own half the county in a few more years at the rate they're going."

"I guess different things matter to different people, Nancy," Marianne defended. "I can remember Uncle Will talking with Mom and Dad about how hard things were when they first came here to farm. He's older. Maybe he needs the security more than you and Tim do."

"Security. Why, Marianne, honey," Nancy confided in a whisper that could be heard on the next farm, "when we sold the creamery to Nestle's we got a nest egg big enough to last us as long as we live."

Harry pulled up then with his mother, and soon after, Carrie called them all in to dinner. Marianne loved them all, she thought, as they sat around the big oak table in the Hanlon dining room. But it was hard to realize that their world had been her world just a few years before.

Will and her father were having a heated discussion with Harry at one end of the table—something about the strawberries Matt had put in.

"But it's a big investment, especially when you consider you really need to pull the old plants and start over every three or four years," Will insisted.

"They're going for a nickel a box, though," Matt reminded him. "Even after I pay off the labor contractor I'm making 30 percent, maybe 40 percent more than I could on lettuce."

Harry nodded thoughtfully. "Diversity," he assured them. "The big mistake a lot of farmers are making right now is putting all their acreage into lettuce. Sure, it does great, but if everybody plants lettuce, pretty soon there's too much lettuce, and the bottom's going to drop out of the price."

Across the table, Ted and Tim were deep into a discussion of the butterfat content Tim's herd was producing, as compared to the test herd at the university at Davis.

Nancy regaled the women about her latest shopping trip to San Francisco and the new furniture she'd ordered. Marianne smiled, realizing that her mother and Irene were as bored as she was by the monologue.

Anna, the doting grandmother, had taken a seat at the kitchen table with the children. Marianne caught their chatter, especially Ellen's tinkling laugh, and she wished she could join them. But . . .

She shrugged the wish away. This was her welcome home party, and these people loved her every bit as much as she loved them. They might not have as much in common as they once had, but they were family. They cared for each other, and they always would.

Adele and Donald came the following evening. Marianne liked Donald immediately. He wasn't at all the type of man she'd have chosen for Adele four years ago; he was surprisingly quiet. Marianne smiled to herself as she thought how lost he'd have been among the teasing, bantering, jabbering crowd of the night before. Not like Paul. Paul would have joined in and probably had them all talking about China in fifteen minutes.

Donald looked so bookish. He even wore glasses. But he adored Adele, and she adored him. They sat in the Hanlon parlor for at least two hours, and rarely took their eyes from each other. Adele chatted with Marianne about San Francisco, and they briefly spoke about China. Donald asked polite questions about the mission work Marianne expected to be doing, and Marianne talked with him about his plans for the high school, now that he was to be the new principal.

Marianne was happy for Adele, but she wondered whether she'd lost her old girlhood chum. That concern vanished the following Saturday, though, when Adele came alone.

"Oh, I do love him so, Marianne," she gushed, just as she had when they were schoolgirls together. "But we couldn't really do 'girl talk' with him here, could we?"

They huddled on the porch swing and whispered and giggled, just as they had when they were sixteen. "If only we'd known you'd be here for the wedding, Marianne. I'd have loved to have you for my maid of honor."

"I haven't worn a party dress and high heels in so long I'd probably fall flat on my face coming down the aisle." Marianne laughed. "Besides, someone has to keep tabs on your flower girl," she added with more than a little touch of pride creeping into her voice.

Adele squeezed Marianne's hand. "She's such a beautiful little girl. How can you bear to go all the way to China and leave her behind?"

"We do what we have to, Adele. I've been away nearly all her life as it is, even if the distance were shorter. Sometimes I think it's better if I am farther away. Seeing her and not being able to claim her, or seeing her for a few days and then having to leave her again, that's what breaks my heart."

"Marianne, I know it still hurts you to talk about it, but there's something . . . I can't help but wonder, even though it's none of my business, and sometimes, when I look at her, well . . . Marianne, who was her father?"

Marianne evaded Adele's question by asking her own. "Do people still talk? I'm afraid even to go out visiting for fear they do. Adele, do they believe what we told them?"

Adele hesitated, and her pause confirmed Marianne's fears. "Can you do anything, please, for Ellen's sake? Don't let her be hurt as she grows up."

"Everyone loves her. I don't think anyone would ever say anything to her. It's just gossip. And I don't think anyone else—no, that isn't true. Sometimes, when Mama looks at Ellen I think maybe she's guessed."

"Gran? Guessed what?" Anna was the one person, next to Ellen, that Marianne wanted most to protect.

"Even strangers comment about it." Adele hesitated. "Marianne, I took Ellen shopping one day, and someone told me what a beautiful daughter I had."

"Surely people don't think . . ."

"People who've been around here all along know that isn't possible. But look at her." Adele studied Marianne's face. "Marianne, Eric went away right after Tim and Nancy's wedding. Ellen was born in March. He's my own brother, Marianne, half-brother anyhow. Please tell me I'm wrong."

Marianne admitted, sadly, what Adele already knew, "Mom and Dad know, Adele, but not another living soul. And no one must ever know, for your mother's sake especially. And you mustn't blame him. He was sick, and he'd been drinking. He was terribly hurt because Nancy married Tim. That was when it happened, right after the wedding."

"When I went to get the others." Adele nodded. "That's what I figured must have happened."

"If you guessed, who else may have? We've tried so hard to keep Ellen from being hurt, and your mother. Were the lies all for nothing? Oh, Adele, what can we do to protect them?"

Adele hugged her. "Nothing. The best thing we can do is nothing. But remember, they're both surrounded by people who love them."

164

The two young women sat quietly in the porch swing for several moments. At last Adele spoke again. "What happened between you and Paul, Marianne? From your letters we all thought you would be getting married this month, too, and then suddenly your mother said he was going to China right away, and you were coming here for a visit. You haven't even mentioned him. Are you joining him in China, or . . ."

"There isn't really anything to say, Adele. Things just didn't work out."

"It wasn't the Salvation Army, was it? You didn't break up because of some fussy old rule of theirs, did you?"

Marianne shook her head. "No, I don't think the Army would have refused us permission, but we never asked for it. Something happened."

Adele opened her mouth to ask another question, looked at Marianne's face, and gave her friend's hand a warm squeeze.

Marianne sighed. "I told him, Adele. Maybe you'll think I'm a fool, but I couldn't marry him without him knowing."

"He did ask you to marry him, then?"

"Oh, yes." Marianne felt her eyes watering. "Adele, I shouldn't have let it go that far. I let him court me. I kept telling myself there was no need to make a fool of myself by telling him something like that when he only wanted to be my friend anyway, but that was just an excuse. I was afraid I'd lose him."

"Of course you were! Marianne, nobody knows but me and your mom and dad. Of course you wouldn't tell every man who took you out a few times."

"I even let him introduce me to his parents," Marianne told her. "No, I should have told him sooner." The swing creaked, and Marianne brushed away a tear. "I was afraid I'd lose him, and I did."

"Oh, Marianne," Adele said softly; they rocked in silence for a few minutes. "Honey, I'm so sorry. Here I've been chattering on and on about my wedding, and not giving a thought to how you've been hurting."

"It's all right, Adele. You have every right to be happy, and I'm happy for you, really I am. Just because it isn't the Lord's will for me to marry Paul doesn't mean your wedding should be any less than perfect."

On the morning of Adele's wedding, Marianne carefully dressed Ellen in her ruffled blue dress and taught her just how to walk down the church aisle scattering rose petals in Adele's path.

She was such a beautiful child, ivory-skinned and rosy-cheeked. Carrie and her daughters had all been taut and lithe, even as children, but Ellen's baby fat never quite left her. "Our little dumpling," Matt called her. She had dimples, instead of the proud jutting McLean chin, and her pale blue eyes opened wide to the world rather than twinkling under long lashes.

Anna sat in the front pew on the aisle next to Harry and his wife. The Hanlons were behind them, so Marianne couldn't see Anna's face. But she saw the beloved head, no longer blonde, but nearly white, turn to smile at the little flower girl. And then she saw that head bow over folded hands as if in prayer.

Deep in her heart, Marianne thought, *she does know. Maybe she doesn't even know she knows, but she does. My little girl has so many people who love her.*

Chapter Eighteen

*M*arianne had loved working in surgery, especially during the summer she'd worked with Paul. But the little dispensary she ran in a back room at the headquarters of the Chinatown Corps was fulfilling, too, in its way. She knew that many of her patients came to her after the Chinese herbalists and acupuncturists had failed, and sometimes she was able to help. She never admitted it to the doctor who oversaw her work, but sometimes the reverse was true.

Chinatown's wooden shacks had burned twenty years earlier, in the great fire that followed the San Francisco earthquake, but the area was still a warren of narrow lanes and overcrowded three- and four-storied brick tenements. Women and children sewed cotton garments, embroidered fine silk, and painted china knick-knacks in windowless basements and on top floors of factories without fire escapes.

But it was a colorful place on the surface. Tourists thronged the shops to purchase the cheap goods made by cheap labor; they ate chop suey, never guessing how the restaurant owners laughed at the white man's strange taste for leftovers; they turned up their noses at the pungent smells of ginger and incense, as well as the smells of garbage and poverty-stricken humanity.

Marianne went into the teeming tenements with Jade. Even when the gospel was not welcome, her nursing skills were. "Oh, Jade," she said with a sigh as they went from one discouraging flat to the next, "they try so hard to keep clean and take care of their children. And they work, constantly, but for such low wages."

"Yes," Jade agreed. "It's like Shanghai, in some ways. But oh, so much better. You think it is poor and crowded here, but Shanghai is twice as poor and crowded. In Shanghai there is often no work at all."

"Do you think it will be better there soon?" Marianne asked thoughtfully. "Dr. Sun seems to have been a good man, and his followers are still gaining ground."

Jade shook her head. "There are always revolutions in China. Sun Yat Sen said good things. He wanted to break the power of the warlords and the wealthy landlords, I guess. I think he would have tried to bring in Western machinery and learning, and that would have helped, maybe. But there are so many people, and they are so set in the old ways. Besides, now that Dr. Sun is dead, his followers are fighting among themselves."

"At least they've stopped binding the girls' feet," Marianne offered. "Isn't that a good sign?"

"It's a little thing, but I guess it is an omen, at least." Jade glanced down at her own feet, in their plain, square-heeled oxfords. "The poorest never bound their daughters' feet anyhow. They couldn't afford the luxury of a child who ate but couldn't work."

"Aren't you lucky, then, that you at least escaped that? It must have been torture."

"It was." Jade shivered. "I knew lots of girls who went through it." She shrugged. "But it was going out of fashion even when I was a girl. The missionaries have had some influence, and the Western businessmen have had even more, I suspect."

"So," Marianne insisted, "if that can change, so can the exploitation—using people to produce cheap goods at cheap prices for big profits, the opium trade, the prostitution."

"I hope so, Marianne. Yes, I pray so, and I know God can save China. But one soul at a time, it will be a long, long battle."

"No doubt you're right about that, Jade, but as useful as the work here is, I'm still eager to get to China and get started."

While Jade worked with Marianne in the little dispensarv and in the tenements, she always seemed to have something else to do when they were invited to one of the surprising number of luxurious apartments hidden away on side alleys. "What's the matter, Jade?" Marianne asked. "Do you think the well-to-do are beyond God's love because of the way some of them treat the poor? They aren't all bad, you know."

"I know," Jade admitted. "Many of the women would change things if they could, and they need the Lord Jesus fully as much as the poor do, maybe more."

"Then why won't you go with me to call on them, Jade? Is it because you used to be a servant there?"

"No, it isn't that, Marianne. I can hold my head up proudly because I have been delivered." She glanced up quickly at the faces around her, and then looked down at the sidewalk as if to hide her face.

Marianne had noticed the gesture before. "You said once that you'd run away. Is that it? Are you afraid of the people you ran away from?" Jade continued to study the paving. "But Jade, this is America. They can't hurt you here."

"Chinatown isn't the America you know, Marianne," Jade insisted. "I know I shouldn't be afraid, because of Jesus. But there are people . . ."

"Are you afraid they'll try to get you back? Jade, slavery is against the law here. They wouldn't dare."

Jade only shrugged and pointedly changed the subject.

Marianne spent her mornings in the dispensary, her afternoons making housecalls, and her evenings at Corps meetings. She didn't have much time for regrets, at least. The wet winter gave way to a sunny spring, and news came from China, to Chinatown at least.

"I wonder why there is so little in the San Francisco papers about what's happening there," Marianne said to Jade one night. "The Chinese language papers are full of news."

"It's only China," Jade responded. "But it does sound as if Chiang and the Kuomintang are winning. They've taken Canton and Wuhan and have forces in Shanghai now."

"There's been a lot of fighting in the north, too, hasn't there?" Marianne could follow the talk of the people she worked with in Chinatown, but she relied on Jade to read the newspapers printed in the new simplified Chinese characters. "Some missionaries have been attacked, I've heard."

Jade nodded. "In Wuhan and in Hangkow. They are toward the south, not near our work." She studied Marianne's face. "You still worry about Paul, don't you?"

Near the end of April word came that the Kuomintang had driven the warlord's forces from Shanghai. There had been bloody riots, Communist-led, they were told, but these had been put down by the new leader of the Kuomintang, Chiang Kai-shek. He might not be a Christian, but American reporters said he was sympathetic to Western Christian ideas. The best news was that he was staunchly anti-Communist, so Shanghai was now safe and in friendly hands.

In May, the Salvation Army sent an officer couple from Peking to open a work in the busy port city among the soldiers. Marianne and Jade prepared to join them.

They arrived on a hot, muggy morning in August. Marianne and Jade had been on deck since sunrise watching rice paddies and tiny thatched farmhouses on the bank of the Yangtze River. "I thought Shanghai was a seaport," Marianne had said to Jade as their ship started up the broad, muddy river.

"It is," Jade told her. "But the city itself is a few miles up on the Whangpo River, where the ground is more stable."

The ship moved slowly against the strong current. Marianne looked from the farm families bent low over their crops to little sampans floating downstream past her. They also passed square-sailed junks, broad beamed and high bowed, with decks jammed full of bales of grain, wooden boxes of all sizes, and people.

The people interested her the most, of course. There were so many of them. Long before they came in sight of the city itself, the land teemed with people. Marianne was used to the fields of the Salinas Valley, where the ten-acre parcels had long since disappeared. A small farm there now was 100, maybe 200 acres. Here each tiny patch seemed to have several people working on it. *How do they grow enough to feed themselves?* she wondered.

The little fishing boats were so thick they had to part so the steamship could pass. "Look, Jade, there seems to be a whole family in each of them." Marianne pointed at one, just a few yards from them. "It looks as if they have bed rolls, and I think I see a little stove, even. Why, they could live right on there."

"They probably do," Jade told her. "Most fishing families have no other home."

It was a sobering thought. "But isn't it too cold in the winter? What about storms?"

Jade shrugged. "When it gets cold, they take their padded winter outfits out of the chest, unless they've had to pawn them. When it rains they put some oiled cloth up on those poles, if they're lucky enough to have any."

"How awful."

"They're better off than the beggars, Marianne. On the streets of Shanghai you will see people who have, at best, a tiny reed shelter. These people at least have a livelihood from fishing."

"And the farmers? How can they support their families on such little pieces of ground?"

"Barely, in a good year." Jade's voice was as impassive as her face. "Now you see why they sell their daughters."

Their ship nosed into the narrower, tributary Whangpo, and the river traffic became even thicker. Jade pointed ahead. "There is Shanghai, just around that bend. You can see the walls of the old city."

"We should be docking soon, then, but I don't see where."

"They will send out sampans to meet us and take us to the Bund," Jade explained. "That's the European section beyond the old city—a different world, really. Clean. Pretty. On the outside, anyhow," she added softly.

Marianne gazed at the mud-brick walls that hid the old city from her for the moment. She sensed that Jade knew all too well what lay behind those walls. But she clearly didn't want to talk about it. *Well, I'll find out soon enough*, Marianne told herself.

The ship rounded the bend, where the crew dropped anchor in the river, and scores of colorful sampans rowed out to ferry the passengers and their luggage to shore. As they waited their turn, Marianne studied the scene before her.

She understood that much of the Shanghai riverfront had been ceded to European governments a generation or more ago. There had been a French Concession, a German Concession, and a British Concession.

The United States had never established a formal governmental agency. Many Americans did business in Shanghai, but they had merged their lands with the British. This area was now called the International Settlement. The newly leased Salvation Army headquarters were within that district too.

Fronting the Bund, the broad, tree-lined street that ran along the riverbank, were the three- and four-storied brick warehouses, offices, and banks from which foreigners had controlled China's imports and exports for nearly a hundred years. The homes of the traders and government officials had wide lawns and verandas that overlooked the river.

The buildings were Victorian in style. *I could almost still be in San Francisco*, Marianne thought, as they boarded one of the sampans. *Except for the people.* The Bund was crowded, like everything else she'd seen in China. There were very few cars though.

The people walking on the street had round faces and dark hair, like Jade. Most of them wore what Marianne described to herself as cotton pajamas, most often blue, and most often soiled and shabby. She recalled Jade's fastidious habits and her comments about the luxury of soap and water.

There were others, the clean ones, who didn't walk. They rode in two-wheeled carts pulled by some of the men in dirty cotton. Some were Europeans or Americans;

many were Chinese. A few were dressed in colorful silk robes, but most wore Western dress.

"It's so crowded, even here," Marianne remarked, as their sampan neared the shore.

"It didn't used to be this way. Back before the Boxer Uprising, I'm told, Chinese weren't even allowed on the Bund," Jade explained. "Even when I was a little girl, not many Chinese came here. But now they are buying businesses themselves." She pointed to some of the signs as they alit from their sampan.

Marianne couldn't read the Chinese characters, but the sign marking the new Hong Kong and Shanghai Bank was written in English as well. Here, at least, the city seemed prosperous. "That should be good news," Marianne commented. "That means more of the wealth of the country will stay here to help the people."

"Not likely," Jade snorted. "There have always been rich Chinese. But sharing the wealth isn't part of the culture, I'm afraid, even since the latest revolution."

Marianne noticed that Jade had pulled her Salvation Army bonnet forward so that it nearly hid her face and that she seemed to be studying the paving stones. But Marianne eagerly tried to take in the entire kaleidoscope at once, even as she looked for the familiar uniforms she expected to meet them. "Oh, there they are." She waved toward the couple who had spotted her at nearly the same instant. "Jade, there's Major and Mrs. Major Douglas."

Marianne was surprised when Major Douglas gestured to some of the men who waited with their rickshaws in a long line along the Bund. The idea of being carried by another human being bothered her. "We aren't that tired, Major. We can walk," she protested.

He smiled. "It's all right, Lieutenant Marianne. They expect it of white men, and would think less of us if we walked. Besides, it's better to pay them for honest work than to force them to beg for food, isn't it?"

"He's right, Marianne," Jade offered, though Marianne noticed Jade, herself, seemed reluctant to climb into the offered chair. "These men earn a few copper coins to feed their families. Otherwise, they would have to beg and send their children out to beg, or worse."

Marianne and Jade mounted the chairs, though both were awkward and uncertain. As one of the men helped Jade into her seat, he saw her face beneath the sheltering bonnet, and Marianne noticed the surprise on his face. As he picked up the long handles of Jade's rickshaw, he turned to his fellow laborers, pointing back at his passenger, and said something Marianne couldn't hear. But she could understand their glances. Obviously they'd never seen a Chinese Salvationist before, but why did they seem angry?

They turned from the parklike Bund up busy Nanking Road, where European women and wealthy Chinese shopped at modern department stores and in tiny cubbyholes displaying gorgeous brocade fabrics and delicate porcelains. Restaurants offered trays of pastries.

A number of the storefronts were tightly shuttered, though lanterns were strung along the edges of their tiled roofs and bright curtains fluttered from open upper windows. Marianne guessed those businesses flourished at night.

Smells of saffron, ginger, and garlic assailed her as well as less exotic smells—of urine, feces, and sweating humanity. She understood why many of the others who rode rickshaws held handkerchiefs to their noses. *But I'm a farmer's daughter and a nurse*, she reminded herself. *I'll get used to it.*

The group of runners and their patrons turned up one narrow street and down another. *I may have to let them carry me*, Marianne thought. *Otherwise, I'll get totally lost.*

Off the main streets she began to see a little of what Jade had warned her about. Down an alley she saw a dozen or so lean-to sheds huddled against a brick wall. They seemed to be made of woven grass, like booths street vendors might build for shelter for a day or so from the sun. But gaunt women and children with distended bellies emerged from them and approached the rickshaws.

"Please." They held out tiny bowls and Major Douglas tossed a few coins into some of them and said something. She couldn't understand all of it, but he seemed to be telling them the coins were a gift from Jesus.

One of the women noticed Jade, and the same astonished look crossed her face that Marianne had seen on the rickshaw bearers. She, too, pointed. Some of the children began to laugh and others to shout. Marianne could make out a few of the words, like "traitor," "slave of foreign dogs," "white man's—," She wasn't sure of the last word, but it wasn't complimentary, she knew. Jade said something to her bearer and hid her face in her hands as he ran off.

I knew there was a lot of resentment of foreigners, Marianne puzzled. *But Jade is Chinese herself. Do they hate her that much just for helping us, or could some of these poor beggars possibly have known her before?*

Jade's bearer was too far ahead for Marianne to ask any questions. But surely, she thought, no one who had ever known Jade could hate her. *I'll ask her about it when we are alone again,* she told herself. In the meantime, the exotic city distracted her from the mystery surrounding her friend.

In some places, Marianne could see to the end of one of the alleys. Then she caught glimpses of dirt embankments covered with barbed wire and, occasionally, rounded structures that looked like the pictures of gun-emplacements she'd seen in newspapers years ago, during the war.

"Yes," the major responded to her query later. "Back in the spring, before Chiang's forces took the city from the Bolsheviks, the International Settlement was seriously threatened. The mobs are under control now, though. There's some resentment of foreigners, still, and some of it deserved, I fear, but we're quite safe here. It isn't wise to venture outside the Settlement alone, of course, but we're trying to begin a limited ministry."

The Salvation Army had rented a neat compound enclosed by high mud walls. Inside the wall was a long, low, tile-roofed brick building. "An infirmary we hope, now that we have a trained nurse," the major told Marianne and Jade.

Opposite it, a nearly windowless, thatched mud shelter was "our orphanage for now, though we hope to build

179

a better building soon." Mrs. Major Douglas's severe military demeanor softened. "There are so many foundlings. We can't rescue more than one in a hundred, but we try."

At the back of the compound were several small cottages made of mud, too, but they had tiled roofs and had been whitewashed. Mrs. Major Douglas, who told them to call her Maddy, explained, "The center one is where the major and I live, and the others house the Chinese Christians who work with us. And here," she opened the door of one of the cottages, "are your quarters."

She had directed her words almost entirely to Marianne. Now she turned somewhat awkwardly to Jade. "Unless you would be more comfortable with the others. Since you're an officer and used to American ways, we thought you'd prefer to stay here, but . . ."

"If you would prefer, I can stay with the other Chinese, Mrs. Douglas."

Mrs. Major Douglas seemed relieved until Marianne protested firmly. "Nonsense. Jade is my coworker, my language teacher, and my best friend too." She stepped into the second of the two small rooms, where their luggage had been stacked. "You take the right side of the wardrobe, Jade, and I'll take the left. Do you want the top dresser drawers or the bottom?"

Chapter Nineteen

*M*arianne and Jade spent most of their time, at first, setting up a small dispensary and clinic, where Marianne, with Jade's help, could offer medicines and bandages to the poor of the city. Word spread quickly that new Westerners had come, who would care for the sick, the injured, and the outcasts without asking any dangerous questions.

Jade fell easily into the routine, but Marianne struggled with the nuances of language and custom. "But when someone does you a kindness, it seems so rude not to say 'thank you,'" she insisted.

"Not to a Chinese," Jade reminded her. "To a Chinese, saying 'thank you' is a way to avoid repaying an obligation. When a Chinese does you a kindness, you await the opportunity and repay the kindness."

"So when I'm going to change a surgical dressing and Grace brings me the bandages, I just nod and smile. But then I help her put away the supper dishes."

"Right," Jade cheered.

"But 'please' is okay?"

"'Please' is fine."

"Then, please, will you go for a walk with me this evening? I feel I've been shut up in this compound ever since we got to Shanghai. I know the nursing is important, but is that the only reason we were sent here?"

"Your nursing skills are badly needed," Jade reminded her.

"But our business is to minister to souls as well as bodies. Surely we don't want to limit it to those who come to us, here."

"But, Marianne, it's still a real ministry. We really can help the girls who come to us. Look at Cherry."

Cherry had come to the compound just a week after Marianne and Jade arrived. Early that morning they had heard the bell that hung by the gate. By the time they were dressed the Major was in the courtyard, surrounded by Chinese servants. A girl no more than thirteen or fourteen years old lay on the pavement. She was obviously in an advanced stage of labor and incoherent.

Marianne knelt by the girl and examined her quickly.

"At least someone cared enough about her to bring her here, instead of just letting her die," the Major muttered. "Is there anything you can do for her?" he asked Marianne.

"I don't know. She's so tiny, and I think the baby is turned cross-wise. Jade, help me get her inside."

Marianne had never performed a Caesarean section; in the United States she would never have been permitted to try. But she had assisted in several, and it was obvious this girl would die if she didn't try.

Sadly, the baby girl was stillborn, but thanks to Marianne's efforts, a lot of prayer, and the tender care and good food given her, the young mother lived.

"Why do you come here?" Cherry had asked Marianne as she changed the surgical dressing a few days later. "Here, it is everyone's dream to go to America."

Jade was right about Marianne's Chinese. It was woefully inadequate, but she struggled to explain to the girl about God and his love.

"The white man's God." Cherry nodded. "He makes the white man wealthy. Some rich Chinese have taken him for themselves, but he isn't for us."

"He's everyone's God, Cherry. Not just the white man's God. He loves everyone."

"Not the poor people. I know. The white missionaries came to the house where I was. They came in fine Western clothes and drank tea with the wives. They talked about this God they call Jesus, but they never saw us. Even when we were in the room, serving the tea and pastries, they never saw us."

Marianne dropped the soiled bandage in a basin and used forceps to pick up a square of clean gauze. "You mustn't judge our God entirely by his followers," she said sadly. "We aren't good enough, but we do try. That's why I'm here. I want to help you, Cherry."

The girl's body healed slowly, and Marianne had many opportunities to talk to her. At last she pulled the sad story from her. A son of the household had used her.

"That is the way it is," Cherry had told her without either shame or anger. "Poor girls are sold to be servant girls, and if the sons like them, they take them." She bit her lip shyly. "I was proud, at first, that he liked me. I hoped he might take me as his third wife, or at least as a concubine."

Marianne caught her breath. "You hoped?"

"Even a third wife or a concubine has a place," she sighed. "But he tired of me when I became big with the child. And then his number one wife, when she heard my screams when the baby wouldn't be born, told the amah to put me out of the house."

"When you were in labor? When you could have been dying?"

"That would have gotten me out of the way. And would have ended my trouble too."

"Someone cared enough to bring you here."

"The gatekeeper, I suspect. He had been kind to me. Once I heard that he had asked for me as a wife for his son, but that was before . . ." Her eyes filled with tears. "Now no one will want me for a wife; I have been ordered out of the house of my master; I have no place to go. Wouldn't it have been better if I had died?"

"You can stay here with us," Marianne had assured her simply. "I will teach you how to care for the sick, and you can help us. And then you, too, will learn that Jesus really is your God."

"Yes," Marianne admitted to Jade. "Cherry came to us, and she's accepted the Lord. She's doing well with her training too. But I want to go out and find the ones who don't get brought here."

"That's not practical, Marianne. The streets of Shanghai aren't safe."

"I know Major Douglas thinks it best that we women not hold street meetings yet, but surely we could visit the markets where the women go."

Jade didn't answer, but Marianne realized her fingers were clenched tightly. "You're still afraid of the people you ran away from, aren't you?"

Jade nodded. "But I must get over it, Marianne. You're right. My fear of going out among the people is hindering my ministry, and yours too."

"I do want to go to the women where they are, Jade, and teach them, and I need your help. You know the language and the culture. But not if it puts you in danger. Maddy has her Bible classes for the ladies. I can help her with those while you stay here, safe, and mind the clinic."

Jade shook her head. "Marianne, you are the nurse. I must put my old fears aside. The clinic should be your first priority, and the teaching mine. Why, the people I am afraid of have probably forgotten all about me by now anyhow. Please pray for me, that I will learn to trust Jesus more."

"I will, Jade." Marianne slipped an arm around her friend's shoulder. "I know Jesus will protect you, but you must do what you think best. Your work here in the compound is important, too, and you should stay here until the Lord gives you peace about going out."

Jade stayed within the compound for a few weeks, working harder than anyone else with the sick who came to them. Her kinship with the people won their confidence. The Chinese girls who sought shelter opened up to her as they seldom did to anyone else, and she led many to Jesus in the quiet nights in the little infirmary.

The Chinese men who came to be patched up after street brawls seemed, at first, to be offended that a Chinese lady would do such work, but they, too, responded to her nursing skill and her witness of the love of the white man's God.

Marianne said nothing more to her about the women's classes, but she had been deeply touched by what Cherry had said about the missionaries who never saw the servants. When, at last, she received permission to teach a group of maids in one of Shanghai's wealthiest homes, Marianne couldn't keep the news from Jade. "Madame Soong!" she reported eagerly. "Madame Soong herself has said we can have a class for her servants, Jade."

"For the servants?" Jade queried. "Just the servants, in their quarters?" Marianne nodded. "Then I will go with you and help."

"Not if it puts you in danger," Marianne protested.

"I'd be safe enough with the servants."

But Marianne noticed that Jade shifted uneasily from foot to foot. "You're still afraid of something, I know. Are you afraid to meet the wives of the well-to-do because you were a servant once, and you don't think you're good enough? You know that's nonsense."

"No, that isn't it." Jade smiled. "I was a servant once, but I know how to sit on those carved chairs in the front parlor sipping tea and nibbling rice cakes too."

"But . . ." Marianne was startled as much by Jade's smile as by her admission. "But you told me you'd been sold into slavery."

"I also told you there were people in Shanghai I'd rather not see again, Marianne. But I'm not likely to meet those people among Madame Soong's serving maids."

"Well . . ." Marianne sensed Jade's continued uneasiness, but she was eager to do what she had come to China to do. "My Chinese really isn't very good, Jade, and Maddy doesn't speak this dialect much better than I do. We get by with the better-educated women—most of them speak a little English anyway—but with the servants we really could use your help, if you think it's safe."

Jade smiled again. "My enemies don't live in the servants' quarters."

"Are you sure?" Marianne asked.

"The Soongs' is a Christian household," Jade said. "The husband and wife have been baptized, and they give generously, I'm told, to support missionary activity. Since she has agreed her servants should hear the gospel, I'm sure Jesus will keep me from harm there."

They were taken from the front gate to an outer parlor where the lady of the house entertained a few guests. She left the other women briefly to welcome Marianne and Jade.

"Take them to the third court," she directed the gatekeeper. She turned to Marianne and Jade. "The women who want to join your class are gathered there. I wish you success."

As she returned to her guests, Marianne noticed one of the elegantly dressed women staring at them, but that wasn't unusual. "Come on," Jade whispered hoarsely, grabbing her arm. "Hurry. We have to get to our new pupils."

Marianne smiled when she saw the group of a dozen or so servant women. Some were no more than children; a couple were wrinkled crones. Most wore what she suspected were their only holiday clothes, clean and neatly mended. They were certainly better off than the women in the streets. Marianne knew they were essentially slaves in the household, but they seemed well treated.

They chattered to one another as they waited, obviously excited about being permitted to listen to the white women who were coming to teach them. She could make out a few words. "Us, slaves, they will teach?"

Someone pointed at Marianne and laughed. "See her hair, the color of sweet potatoes."

Jade still kept her head bowed, but they gestured toward her anyhow. "Like us. From America, but she looks like us."

Jade told them that she was like them. "I was a servant in Shanghai once," she explained. "But God, the one true God, made a miracle for me, and I was taken to America. Now I have come back to tell you about this God and his son, Jesus."

Jade was coming out of her shell, Marianne realized. Her dark eyes glowed as she told them of this God who cared about people and wanted to help them. Most of the women listened politely, though the younger girls seemed more interested in Marianne's red hair and their strange clothing.

Jade finished her testimony, and, as they had agreed, Marianne rose to tell the women about the Salvation Army and the clinic. "We will come back and teach you more about Jesus. We'd like to teach you other things, too, about how to care for yourselves and your children so that you will have less sickness."

"Why do you try to teach us? We are only women and too stupid to learn," someone protested.

"God loves women too." Marianne smiled. "Jade and I are women, and we have learned these things. So you can learn too."

Heads shook in disbelief, but Marianne continued. "Do you know where our infirmary is?"

There were a few nods.

"You can come there. Anyone can, if you are sick or injured or alone. We want to help you and your children."

"Our rickshaw men will be waiting for us," Jade reminded Marianne, as the women surrounded them asking questions. "And if we keep the women too long from their work, we may not be permitted to come back."

"Next week," they assured the women as they left.

"I thought it went fairly well," Marianne said to Jade as they retraced their way through the interlocking court-yards.

"Not bad, for a beginning. At least they listened," Jade agreed. "I think they suspect we're Communists though."

"Oh, no. They mustn't think that."

"Why not, for now at least?" Jade smiled at Marianne's horror. "Communism sounds terrible to us because we understand how it is opposed to the gospel. But to them, Communists are just another faction—more soldier-bandits, offering land and food to everyone, and then stealing it for themselves."

"And Chiang's troops, are they any better?"

Jade put a finger to her lips. "Not here. This isn't the place to discuss such things."

They climbed into the waiting rickshaws. For some time their two runners jogged side by side, but suddenly Marianne saw Jade's bearer dart down a crowded alleyway. "Stop," she called. "Wait. Where are they going?" But the man who pulled her paid no attention to her cries. He doggedly trotted through the teeming streets and silently deposited Marianne at the gate of the Salvation Army compound.

Marianne hustled inside and looked around the compound. "Have you seen Jade?" she inquired. "Is she back?"

"Didn't she come with you?" Maddy Douglas replied.

Marianne told her how the rickshaw bearer had run off. "Do you think they could have kidnapped her for ransom?" Marianne grasped at the hope that Jade was merely one more hostage, easily redeemed in lawless Shanghai. "The bandits do seem to think all white men are rich."

"Oh, my, I hope not," Maddy replied. "Probably her bearer just took another route and missed his way."

"Well, I hope she turns up soon," Marianne continued. "You know, Jade has been afraid of something, or someone, ever since we arrived in Shanghai."

Maddy nodded. "And with some reason. Marianne, did anything unusual happen at the Soongs'?"

"No, not really." Marianne suddenly recalled Jade's reaction to the stare of the guest. "Oh, Maddy, I think she

190

may have recognized someone, a guest of Madame Soong."

"Dear God, help us! Oh, Marianne, we must pray for her. If someone there recognized her, she could be in great danger."

"And it's my fault, Maddy," Marianne confessed. "I made light of her fears and urged her to go out."

Maddy patted Marianne's shoulder. "You mustn't blame yourself, dear. We all thought the Soong household was safe enough."

Marianne tried to concentrate on her nursing duties, but when she had checked on all of her patients, Jade had still not appeared at the compound. Major Douglas gathered his coworkers for prayer. "Please, Lord, watch over your servant Jade and protect her from her enemy."

"Isn't there something we can do?" Marianne asked him when the prayers were finished. "Notify the police; send some of our servants out to ask questions?"

"If there is no word by morning, I will go to the Police Commissioner and see what I can do," he promised, but it seemed to Marianne that he had already given up hope.

"You know what Jade was afraid of, don't you?" she persisted. "And you think something terrible has happened to her."

"She has a powerful enemy in Shanghai," Major Douglas admitted. "She should never have been sent here."

"I begged her to go with me, sir. I knew she was terrified, but I wanted to go, and I persuaded her to go with me. I should have known she had good reason."

191

"She didn't want you burdened with her fears, Marianne. And she believed Jesus would protect her. We have to believe that too." He bowed his head again, as if offering another prayer. "Now I think we should all try to get some rest."

Chapter Twenty

*J*ade did not come back. In every spare moment Marianne prayed. *Oh, God, forgive me for not understanding the danger, and oh, dear God, protect her; keep her safe; bring her back to us, please, dear Jesus.*

But Marianne had very few spare moments. Refugees crowded the infirmary. She saw many frightened runaway girls. With the city overrun with soldiers, there were even more castaway girls. And there were the babies. Cherry took Jade's place going with Marianne to look for the babies.

Baby girls, in China, were often a burden and even a shame to the poorer families. Distraught mothers often brought their infant girls to the International Settlement, where they had heard white people would take them in and care for them. Every morning several dirty, cotton-wrapped bundles could be found abandoned in the filthy alleys.

The first time Marianne had gone out in the early morning, she'd handed the first tiny, cold form to Jade, saying, "We'll take it back and at least give it a decent burial." But soon she realized their arms couldn't be wasted on the dead. Someone else would have to bury them. For every now and then one of the little bundles would twitch, or a hungry wail would come from within the ragged padded cotton. These, the living, they took back to the compound.

Now Marianne combined these rescue missions with her search for her friend. As she walked the narrow streets, as she gathered her babies, as she offered medical care and words about Jesus to the women and children of the streets, she asked questions. "A Chinese woman called Jade, who dresses like I do . . . Have you seen her?"

One cold, drizzly morning in January, as she and Cherry were returning to the compound, they were stopped by an elderly Chinese woman. She spoke no English, but Marianne understood enough Chinese to know that she wanted them to follow her. "No, no," Cherry protested. "She may work for one of the robber gangs. Don't go with her."

The woman gestured frantically. "Stay here if you want to," Marianne told the trembling girl. "I have to find out what she wants."

Cherry followed, as unwilling to wait alone as she was to go along with Marianne. The old woman led them to one of the heavily shuttered, lantern-festooned buildings that Marianne had learned were Shanghai's better brothels. Her stomach churned with fear.

Marianne knew it was dangerous to go inside, but it might be just the kind of opportunity she had prayed for since she arrived in Shanghai. Would there be a woman inside who needed medical help, maybe even one who wanted to learn about Jesus? Or maybe, she dared hope, someone had word about Jade. *I ignored Jade's fears*, she told herself. *Now I must do everything I can to rescue her.*

The lower floor was dark, closed tightly against the daylight. Marianne could see that it was lavishly furnished. Brocaded draperies hung over the windows; bright tiles covered the floor; and the walls were papered with delicate landscape paintings on rice paper.

The old woman maneuvered stealthily past dainty gilded tables and chairs. She held a finger to her lips and glanced from side to side as she led them to a narrow back staircase. Satisfied that the lower floor was deserted, she took them upstairs and knocked discreetly on a door that opened off the dark hallway. Cherry's eyes were wide with fright. Marianne trembled, but she prayed silently that God would give her courage.

"Ah, you came." The slender woman, whose heavily powdered and rouged face hid her age, whispered in stilted English. "Come inside, quickly. The others will still be sleeping."

Cherry's eyes darted around the room, but Marianne watched the woman who sat on a carved teak bed that nearly filled the small space. "Do sit down." She gestured to an ornately carved straight-backed chair. *She's certainly courteous*, Marianne thought, as she took the offered seat.

"You must wonder why I sent for you." When Marianne nodded, she continued softly. "You are the American lady who looks for the Chinese friend?"

"You know something about Jade! Tell me, is she all right?"

"I suspect not."

Marianne's heart sank. "You suspect. You don't know, then."

"I have heard a little gossip, that is all. But I knew her several years ago. She was my friend." The woman turned her head toward the door and seemed pleased that Cherry had stationed herself there. "Did you know that Jade knew places like this?"

Jade had only told Marianne she had been sold as a child. She'd assumed her friend had been a household slave, but now she realized that there had been hints. "Not exactly," she answered. "I knew she'd had a hard life here, but she didn't want to talk about it."

"Are you shocked? Western women often are. Jade was a slave here; we all are. But there are worse lives."

Marianne wondered how that could be. "She was afraid to come back to Shanghai. That's why, isn't it? Do you think someone kidnapped her and . . ." It was too awful to think about. "And took her back?"

The woman shook her head. "They would not want her back now. She is too old and ruined. No, I fear worse than that." She sighed, and Marianne was afraid of what she would say next. "Jade was favored. A man took her from our house to his own home."

"As his slave?"

"Oh, no. She found great favor. She lived in his great mansion as his number three wife."

"His wife!" Marianne could scarcely believe that Jade had kept such a story to herself. "So that's why he took her to San Francisco," she said softly.

"I heard that he took her to America with him for his pleasure. And I heard that she ran away."

"That would be when she went to the Salvation Army for help. I met her soon after that," Marianne explained. "So it's her husband she's been afraid of."

"She shamed him. Do you understand what that means here for a wife who has received a name, a position, rich gifts, to run away from her husband?"

"I can guess." Marianne shivered. She'd seen women beaten to death, or nearly so, for less.

"To come back here without her meant great loss of face. He would make her pay for her insolence if he found her."

"Do you think he found her? Have you heard that he found her?" Though Marianne knew Jade was probably dead already, she prayed, again, for her safety.

"Please, I have heard only rumors, the talk of servants. It is said that the man's number one wife saw her one day and had her taken away to await the husband's return from a business trip."

"Then she could still be alive." Marianne grasped at hope. "Tell me who the man is. I will tell the police and they will go to the wife and question her."

"I dare not say it." The woman stood. "I have said enough, and too much, already. I sent for you to tell you what I have heard, and to tell you to stop asking questions

197

about Jade. The man is too powerful. Even you, an American, are not out of his reach. Tell no one you saw me, or he will kill me as well. Please, I urge you because you are Jade's friend and, for her, I want to help you. Do not meddle in our affairs. It will only hurt you."

She opened the door, and Cherry, after carefully inspecting the hallway, started to leave. But Marianne loitered. "You have done me a great kindness, telling me this. I believe my God, who is Jade's God, too, will protect us all. If you feel you are in danger, please come to me, to the Salvation Army compound. We can keep you safe there."

"A Chinese, a 'Sing-Song' girl? No, you don't want me there."

"We are here to help anyone who needs our help. That is why I came to China and why Jade came back in spite of her fears. Besides, you are Jade's friend, and she is one of us. Please come."

"If I hear any more of Jade, I will send word to you there. Now, go. The other women will be awakening soon."

Marianne and Cherry hurried on through the crowded streets. They were breathless when they arrived at the compound and quickly stepped inside. Marianne wanted to tell the Major what she had learned so he could report it to his friends in the police. But there was no time. As they slipped through the gate they found the courtyard crowded, mostly with women and children.

"Refugees, from the north," someone muttered. "There's been fighting there."

198

Most of the people were in rags. Many of them were injured. Marianne hurriedly scrubbed and began binding the wounds of the newcomers.

Refugees had been drifting into Shanghai and to the Salvation Army compound as long as she'd been there, but this was not a handful of stragglers. Most of them had already had medical treatment, Marianne realized.

"Marianne, thank God you are here," Major Douglas called from across the courtyard. "These people need medical help. There's a girl burning up with fever, most of the men and children have burns or bullet wounds, and a woman is about to have her baby, I think."

As she hurried to the infirmary, she brushed against a woman she had assumed was Maddy Douglas, since she wore a Salvation Army uniform. But now Marianne realized she was a stranger. She must have come with the refugees.

"Barbara, Lieutenant Barbara Cole." The woman introduced herself in a clipped British accent.

"Are you a nurse?" Marianne asked quickly.

"Sorry; no such luck. I know a little first aid, though, and I can follow orders."

"I just thought . . ." Marianne was inspecting the sling that supported a little boy's broken arm. "You've done a very good job. From the dressings I thought these people had had professional help."

"As a matter of fact, they did, but it was several days ago. Our doctor did what he could for them, but he was injured himself. His hands were burned trying to save our infirmary," she explained. "So he bribed a soldier with an army truck to bring the sickest and those who needed surgery here."

Marianne's felt as if her heart had jumped into her throat. *It couldn't be,* she thought. "I didn't know there were any Salvation Army doctors around here," she said, trying to sound only mildly interested.

"Doctor Cameron came to China about a year ago. He's been working a hundred miles or so north of here, where my partner, Kate, and I had started a women's work."

"Captain Doctor Cameron? Not Paul Cameron?" Why was she trembling so? Marianne asked herself. She hadn't seen him in nearly two years after all. There was nothing left between them.

"Why yes," Barbara answered. "Do you know him?"

"I used to." Marianne struggled to calm herself. She ached for news of Paul, but the refugees in the courtyard needed all her attention. "Can you help me get these people settled into our infirmary? Most of the wounds seem to need cleaning and redressing."

Barbara smiled broadly as one of the Chinese servants brought steaming hot water and strong lye soap. "I haven't seen soap in weeks. I can make good use of this," she told Marianne. "I think you have a baby to deliver."

They all worked late into the night. Though she was exhausted, Marianne slept little. Paul was not far away, and he was hurt. Jade might still be alive, too, she thought, but maybe worse than dead. *Oh, God, take care of them,* she prayed.

As the dawn began to light her room, she was up, dressed, and out into the courtyard. The refugees who had slept there were stirring, too, and Maddy Douglas was ladling out bowls of rice gruel for them. As Marianne passed her on the way to the infirmary, she spoke softly. "I've had some information about Jade. I need to talk to the Major as soon as possible."

"Good news?" Maddy kept ladling as she talked to Marianne in English. "Does someone know where she is or who took her?"

"Maybe who took her, though not where she is, or if she is safe," Marianne told her quickly, as she edged past extra cots and into the women's ward of the infirmary. The new mother nursed her baby while a toddler, two or three years old, sat on the foot of her cot slurping thin rice gruel. Beyond her, a waif lay motionless on a cot in the corner. Marianne felt her hot forehead and went for cool water. *I must get her fever down,* she told herself, *and then there are the wounded men to check on.*

"Grace," she called to one of the Chinese nursing helpers, "you and Cherry will have to see that everyone gets breakfast and that beds are made." She took the basin of water back into the ward and began to bathe the feverish girl.

After the girl's forehead had cooled, Marianne took a packet of sterile bandages from a closet and went to tend the men with infected bullet wounds. But Barbara had gotten there before her.

She looked up at the sound of Marianne's step and smiled. "I hope you don't mind that I've made myself at home in your clinic."

"Are you kidding? You look like an angel to me, sent straight from God himself." Marianne turned back the blanket that covered a moaning man and spoke to him, but he didn't seem to comprehend the Shanghai dialect she'd learned from Jade. She hoped he understood enough to know she was there to help. As she began to snip away the blood-soaked bandages, she let herself ask about Paul.

"You were with Dr. Cameron at a village that was attacked, then."

"Not exactly attacked. The local warlord's mercenaries overran our clinic in their retreat. They took all our food and medicine, so we decided I should bring some of our patients here. That one was wounded trying to keep them out of our storeroom." She nodded toward the man Marianne was tending.

"Dr. Cameron insisted on staying behind to do what he could for the people who were still in the villages," Barbara continued, "so Kate stayed to help him. Did you say yesterday that you knew Dr. Cameron?"

Barbara guessed almost immediately just how well Marianne had known Paul and smiled. "You know how it is. A nice, good-looking doctor arrives. Well, I may be a soldier for the Lord, but I'm a woman, too, and naturally Kate and I started wondering if, maybe, the Lord had sent him for one or the other of us. But it was obvious he wasn't interested."

Marianne dropped her eyes, afraid to ask any more questions.

"He'd kid around, you know, but underneath he seemed hurt," Barbara was said. "Once one of the Chinese workers told him that he should pray for a good wife, and he said something funny. He said, 'He sent someone, and I pushed her away.' We wondered if he meant he'd left someone behind because he was coming to China." Barbara looked at Marianne. "But it wasn't that simple, was it?"

Marianne shook her head and started to move on to the next patient. "Marianne, he's smart. He'll manage to survive. And I hope and pray everything works out for you two."

After that Marianne questioned every group of refugees that straggled in. One or two mentioned hearing of a white doctor with burned hands. He'd been seen in a village; he had tended wounded along a highway. "But if he's back there, he hasn't got a chance. Between the warlord's bandits, who'd rob their own mother, and the Bolsheviks, who kill anyone who doesn't agree with them, and the crazy mobs, who blame all their troubles on foreigners, well, if he hasn't turned up here by now, he won't."

Marianne worried silently about Paul and about Jade. She wanted to share her fears for Paul with Barbara, but how could she? He'd left her behind, ashamed of her shame. She had no claim on him, so she shared her fears only with the Lord.

She continued to ask questions about Jade, despite the "Sing-Song" girl's warning. Less than a week had passed when the compound was awakened just before dawn by the clanging of its bell. Though the servants hurried, they found no one standing outside—only a fragile woman, bruised and broken, crumpled against the gate.

When Marianne reached her, the major was already opening the high collar of her plum-colored silk *cheong sam*. A woman, an expensively dressed woman. There were no open wounds, Marianne saw, but the woman's breath came in short, strangled gasps. Marianne bent over her and opened the gown further. There were no marks on her neck, but her sunken chest was a mass of livid bruises. "Kicked?" Marianne queried.

"Systematically beaten, more likely." Major Douglas shook his head sadly. "Undoubtedly bleeding internally. I doubt we can do much for her, but . . ." He signaled to the servants.

They lifted her onto a stretcher to move her inside, but as they did, she groaned and lifted her hand to grasp Marianne's sleeve. "The Christian soldier-lady."

Marianne leaned closer. The hand reached the red emblem on her collar. "Jade's friend?"

Marianne recognized her then, the "Sing-Song" girl who had known Jade. "We're Jade's friends, and your friend," she told the woman. "You're safe now."

The woman's head moved from side to side as she tried to speak. "No, I go to my ancestors."

"You mustn't say that," Marianne protested. "We're going to help you."

"No." It was scarcely even a whisper, and her fingers pleaded for Marianne to lean closer. "Jade . . ."

"Jade? Jade would want you to let us help you."

"Jade is gone. Her husband . . ."

Marianne tried not to believe her. "You must have faith in God, Jade's God."

204

"Jade's God could not save her from the anger of that one. He had her strangled and thrown to the rats."

Marianne's heart rejected the words. "You can't know that. You must have faith."

"My servant saw," the woman gasped. "Jade was killed." The woman had to stop, to gasp for enough precious air to finish what she had to say. "The servant who saw said she died well. She spoke of her God, but he did not save her." There was a rattle in the woman's chest, and Marianne knew she would speak no more.

Jade. Her heart sank. She had dared to hope. But Jade had died with Jesus' name on her lips. Marianne wept for her friend's pain, and for her own loss. *Jade dead and her friend too. If only I hadn't urged her to go with me.* But somehow, she took comfort, too, in knowing. "Jade is with Jesus," she told Major Douglas.

Chapter Twenty-One

She could not grieve long, she knew. The sick and injured kept arriving, and Barbara, as much help as she was,
couldn't take Marianne's place. But Marianne could steal
a little while, a few minutes to weep for her friend, and
for her friend's friend. She went to the little cottage she
now shared with Barbara, and knelt by her bed. Though
her heart ached for Jade, it was Paul she found herself
praying for. "Oh, God, watch over him out there in the
country. Please, God, deliver him from this madness."

She rose from her knees, slipped into a fresh white
uniform, and headed for the infirmary. More refugees
must have arrived, she thought, glancing around the busy
courtyard.

Inside, Barbara was talking to someone. Both had
their backs to her, and at first Marianne did not recognize
the tall, slender man whose black hair was touched with
gray. He stooped slightly with weariness, and he wore the
shabby blue padded cotton the coolies wore. "Thank God

he's kept you safe and brought you here," Barbara was saying.

"You can't be one half as glad to have me here as I am to be here," the tall man answered.

Marianne's feet seemed frozen to the floor. Her throat felt paralyzed. Her eyes blurred so she could scarcely see him as he turned around and recognized her.

"Marianne, oh, Marianne, is it really you, here, now?" He started toward her, arms outstretched, and then, abruptly, stopped. "Marianne." He seemed suddenly shy, feeling for words. "Marianne, are you all right? How long have you been here? Are you really here or am I hallucinating?"

"Paul." Was there a hunger in his eyes to match hers? Or did she only see what she wanted to see? "Thank God you're safe. We heard such terrible things from the refugees."

He didn't take his eyes from her, but his arms dropped, and she saw that his fingers, those beautiful, long, lean surgeon's fingers, were scarred. He self-consciously put his hands behind his back.

"You were hurt—Barbara told us your hands were burned." It wasn't what she wanted to say, but did he want to hear more?

"Stupid, really." He tried to force a grin, and almost succeeded. Thank God he could still look disaster in the face and laugh at it, she thought. "I tried to put out a fire with them."

"Dr. Cameron may not be able to do much surgery until his hands heal," Barbara said. "But I've been telling him how welcome he is here, anyhow."

"Yes, very welcome." Her own words sounded so hollow to Marianne. Did he have any idea how welcome he was? she wondered. Did he care? Except for his first, impulsive gesture, he was being most impersonal, she tried to tell herself. But so was she. After all, they were standing in the middle of a clinic full of patients.

"I understand you two are old friends." Barbara smiled. "I can take care of things here for a little while, if you'd like to go somewhere and talk."

They looked at each other awkwardly, as if they had just met. Someone in the next room screamed out in pain, and Cherry came to the door. "Lieutenant Marianne, they just brought in a baby. It is most awfully sick, I think."

Paul sighed and followed Marianne into the other ward. "We'll talk later, Marianne."

But she saw a tenderness in his eyes when he looked at her. Despite the tragedy surrounding her, Marianne dared to hope. "Yes, Paul. We'll talk later."

After Marianne took care of the sick child, she slipped outside. Her eyes drifted around the busy courtyard as she blinked at the bright sunshine and, remembering the news brought by the dead "Sing-Song" girl, blinked back tears too.

But Paul was here. *No.* She fought back the hope that surged against her reason. Thank God he was safe, but that didn't mean he had changed. She hadn't. Ellen was still her child; in the eyes of society, and in his, she was still a fallen woman.

208

She heard soft footsteps, and felt his hesitant touch on her shoulder. "Red." He whispered the nickname she'd hated at first. It sounded now like the most tender of endearments. "Red, do you know you are a miracle? I was so sure I'd lost you forever."

They were alone in the crowded court, she realized, just as they'd been alone so often among the crowds in San Francisco.

"Marianne, is it too late? Please tell me it isn't too late for me to beg you to forgive my stupid, stupid pride."

"Paul, please," she whispered to him. "You've been through so much. We both have. It's been a year and a half. We're not the same people we were then."

"I'm not," he said firmly. "Thank God I'm not. But I do still love you. I always loved you. Truly I did, but I was stunned, confused, and, yes, proud."

Oh how she wanted to believe what he was saying now, but how could she forget what he had said then, when they'd parted? Barely conscious of the Chinese who crowded the courtyard, she started to walk away, back to a shady corner beside her cottage.

Paul followed. Hidden from view, he lifted her chin in his hands. "Can't you see when you look into my face that I've always loved you? I never stopped loving you."

"Paul, don't. I can't bear to hear this. Paul, I said we'd both changed, but . . ."

"Marianne, no! You can't have found someone else. I know you loved me; you must still love me."

The words forced their way out against her better judgment. "I love you. That will never change. But the other will never change either. My past . . ."

"Hang your past!" It was a hoarse, harsh whisper, almost a groan. His arm circled her waist, and she let him draw her close. He looked down at her upturned face. "Oh, God . . ." She realized it was, indeed, a prayer. "Oh, how I love you, Marianne Hanlon." His lips found hers, brushed them lightly, then pressed them hungrily.

She returned his passionate embrace. She was as hungry for his touch as he for hers. It could have been a minute, or an hour. At last their bodies parted, though their hearts were still one.

"Now I know you still love me," he murmured. "Can you forgive me, too, for hurting you so?"

"I was hurt, Paul, terribly hurt, but so were you. It wasn't your fault, or mine either. It was someone else, a long, long time ago."

He nodded, slowly. "At first I blamed you for leading me on, deceiving me, like I believed you must have led him on." She flinched at the words, but he stroked her hair as he continued. "And I had been hurt, too, before, by someone else."

He bit his lip, as if to stop himself from speaking of his own past. "I must have written you a hundred letters, Marianne, but I couldn't bring myself to mail them. I told myself I wanted a wife like Rose Cameron, above reproach. Not a woman like . . ." The phrase dangled in midair. "I longed to beg your forgiveness, but I felt that my dream had been betrayed—not by you, my dearest, but by, what? Fate?"

He seemed to be groping for the right words. "Marianne, part of me knew you had to have been innocent, but another part believed that old 'conventional wisdom.'"

She nodded and whispered the words: "A good soldier for the Lord must have a helpmate who is pure, and good girls don't get raped."

"All my life I'd believed that, darling. Even so, I wanted to forgive you. I even told myself I could have forgiven you, if you'd only asked. But instead, you'd made an excuse. You told me you'd been raped. And 'good girls' didn't let that happen."

The old fear started to return, and Marianne started to pull away, but Paul's hands gripped hers and held her. "I know I never heard you out, but I'm asking you to be better than me."

She let him draw her close again. "It wasn't just you, Marianne. Maybe if I tell you about her it will help you to understand." His arm still circled her slender body. "I never knew her, but she came between us, even so."

She felt the comfort of his embrace. "Paul, I've wondered sometimes, these past two years, if confession is always best."

"Me too." He almost laughed, almost cried. "But it is. It wasn't your confession that tore us apart, Marianne. It was my pride, my demand for a wife who was an ideal, even an idol. But it was an old bitterness, too, Marianne, against a woman who may have deserved my bitterness no more than you did. I hated her, and some of that hate turned against you."

She didn't understand—a woman he'd never known, but still hated? But it didn't matter. If what Eric had done didn't matter to him, this strange woman didn't matter to her.

"She wasn't like you," he whispered. "She abandoned her child. She was my mother."

Marianne started to protest, but he put a finger to her lips once more. "The woman who gave birth to me. I was adopted by the Camerons," he explained. "I grew up hating that woman, but these past months . . ."

He shuddered, then, and Marianne's caressed his brow. "Oh, Paul."

He sighed, softly. Though he still held her hands in his own, he seemed to draw himself away, just a little. "Then I got caught up in the revolution. I saw things, did things . . . I learned about real life." His voice broke.

His hands were trembling. "Marianne, you're what kept me alive these past few months. The thought that somehow, some way, I had to tell you I understood at last."

He faced her squarely and his eyes met hers. "I shot a man out there, Marianne." She gasped, but he went on quickly. "That isn't a confession, my beloved. I did it to protect a girl, an innocent girl. And all I could think of was that I wished I could have been there to protect you."

She started to speak, then, but he interrupted. "Marianne, I know you, and I love you."

He held her once again, stroking her bright hair. "Yes, I've seen how women are treated here," he murmured. "And I know now that it isn't just here. I know, now, that women *can* be victims, totally innocent victims."

His words broke away the last little bit of the shell she'd built around her heart that summer so long ago. "It was my uncle," she said softly.

"Shhh," Paul soothed. "You don't have to explain."

"But I want to, Paul. I want to say it, once, and then put it behind me forever."

He held her gently, and she felt so safe in his arms. "It was my mother's stepbrother," she told him. "Eric had been hurt, gassed in the war, and then lost his girl to his best friend. He was on morphine, I think, and then, at their wedding he got drunk."

Paul's lips brushed her cheek, but he listened without a word as she let go of the terrible memory. "He went away right afterward, and no one has heard from him since. He never knew about Ellen."

Paul's lips found hers as she finished. They sat close together in the shadows. It was a long time before Paul spoke. "And I so nearly lost you because I wouldn't listen. I blamed you then, but now I know that what happened to you made you the woman I love so much."

He sighed as his arm tightened about her once more. "And God is so good. He's given me a second chance. Will you give me a second chance too? Will you marry me, Marianne?"

She hesitated, just as she had that evening in San Francisco, but there was no secret between them now. There was only joy, a joy so overwhelming that, for an instant, she couldn't speak. She found his eyes with hers, and the words came. "Paul, I love you, as I always have. And I have never wanted anything on earth as much as to be your wife."

About the Author

Jean Grant was born in Michigan but has lived most of her life in northern California. She earned her bachelor's degree from the University of California at Berkeley, and has worked for more than thirty years as a clinical laboratory technologist.

Grant's first novel was The Revelation. Her articles and short stories have appeared in such publications as Evangelical Beacon, Mature Living, Home Life, Seek, and Power for Living. The Promise of Peace follows Grant's first book in the Salinas Valley Saga, The Promise of the Willows.

The Salinas Valley Saga continues with

Book Three

The Promise of Victory

છ

Coming in Spring 1995